Studying Scarlet

A New Sherlock Holmes Mystery

(an unauthorized parody)

Studying Scarlet

A New Sherlock Holmes Mystery

(an unauthorized parody)

Craig Stephen Copland

Note: Both the novel and the movie *Gone with the Wind* are under copyright protection. This book, *Studying Scarlet,* is a parody and as such protected under Fair Use.

The characters of the Sherlock Holmes stories and the story *A Study in Scarlet,* are in the public domain.

Published by:
Conservative Growth
1101 30th Street NW
Washington, DC 20007

Cover design by Rita Toews

ISBN 1500955736
ISBN-13 978-1500955731

DEDICATION

With apologies to two great storytellers:
Arthur Conan Doyle and Margaret Mitchell.

CONTENTS

ACKNOWLEDGMENTS

I discovered both *Gone with the Wind,* and *The Adventures of Sherlock Holmes* while a student at Starlet Height Collegiate Institute in Toronto. My English teachers – Bill Stratton, Norm Oliver, and Margaret Tough – inspired me to read and write. I shall be forever grateful to them.

My colleagues in the Oakville Writers Group endured the drafts of the various chapters of the story and made valuable suggestions. My dearest and best friend, Mary Engelking, read several drafts, helped with whatever historical and geographical accuracy may be present, and made insightful recommendations for changes to the narrative structure, characters, and dialogue.

For the very idea of writing a new Sherlock Holmes mystery I thank the Sherlockian Society of Toronto, known to members as the Bootmakers. They posted a story contest for such a task with the proviso that boots had to play a significant role in the narrative. And so they do.

CHAPTER ONE – YOUR MOMMA

Our beloved Queen Victoria passed away a year ago. All of England, indeed the entire Empire was saddened, but there was a universal feeling that *the old girl had done it well.*

Throughout the Empire a pall, a lethargy had descended. The old order had changed, but the new one to which it would yield its place had not yet begun.

From the poor level of our Baker Street Irregulars all the way to the earls and lords of the land, we simply waited, wondering what the new era would be like. The Prince of Wales, the heir apparent, was no longer a dashing playboy prince. He had become a portly, bearded sixty year old grandfather and all of his subjects agreed that he had finally grown up and was ready to take his rightful role as the head of the greatest empire the world had ever known. In June of 1902 all of the crowned heads of the world gathered in London for the coronation. Half a million citizens were given free dinners and tins of chocolates as part of the celebration only to have the event itself postponed because Albert Edward was ill with a severe pain in his gut.

Now, in early August, he was feeling better and on Saturday would be crowned king at Westminster Abbey with the world's ambassadors standing in for their kings and queens who could not wait around. Even without them, all was well with the world.

My health, so damaged in Afghanistan, had fully recovered. My medical practice had expanded following my purchase of the files of the aging surgeon in Paddington whose affliction with St. Vitus dance had led his patients to seek alternative care. This connection, added to my military pension, was providing me with a solid income of well over three hundred pounds a year. I was rising early, greeting each day with resolute happiness. I was engaged to be married this fall for the third time and was quite certain that together with my lovely wife we would enjoy life until our days together on the earth were done. I could not have been more content.

Sherlock Holmes could not have been more miserable. Without a truly creative criminal with whom to match wits, without any unusual nefarious puzzles to be solved, Sherlock Holmes was indulging overly often in his dangerous seven percent solution and complaining about the petty and utterly predictable cases that had been presented to him for the past year.

From time to time I would hum a few lines from our dear friends Bill Gilbert and Artie Sullivan that I knew would rouse him from his sullenness:

When the enterprising burglar's not a'burglring
When the cut throat isn't occupied in crime
He loves to hear the little brook a-gurgling
And listen to the merry village chimes

Holmes would be sure to respond with "Blast it, Watson, if you must be humming tunes from the stage could you not at least remember something from that infernal nonsense *Pinafore!*"

"Yes, of course, my dear Holmes," I would reply, "but you must admit that our times are splendid , truly the *best of times*, are they not?"

Mind you there was still much crime in London. On the hour it seemed someone's house would be broken into. Somebody would rob a shop or flog a cabbie for his fares. Almost every day someone would be murdered. In the past week alone three men had been murdered in different parts of London, all by garroting. The newspapers were trying to create a panic, warning citizens about *the mad garrotters.* Years earlier they had done the same and caused a panic that swept the city. Such morbid fears about evil murderers had a wonderful effect on the sale of newspapers. The barons of Fleet Street had proven that again quite recently with the salubrious stories of the infamous Jack the Ripper. But these were all just normal, run-of-the-mill crimes; nothing truly, ingeniously, diabolically evil and sufficient to warrant the intense energy of London's most famous detective.

"No, my dear Watson, we do not live in splendid times. We live in very dangerous times, *the worst of times*," remonstrated Holmes. "The Empire is crumbling. The Americans are eating into our trade, and the Germans into our naval superiority. Britain is forming all sorts of unholy alliances with unpredictable countries. The Boers gave our army a thorough run for it and the world cheered them on. Some youth tried to murder the Prince and the Belgian authorities let him walk away. Anarchists are on the move everywhere. They are not murderers of the usual garden variety that kill for money or jealousy. They are fanatical in their beliefs and intent on mayhem and destruction of the established order.

"Yet none of these cases have come to me Watson. Those sorry chaps at Scotland Yard treat every death as if it were just one more unsolvable murder, and I receive nothing but the most trivial of clients wanting help with the most trivial of problems. Look at this, Watson," he snapped as we, or at least I, enjoyed Mrs. Hudson's breakfast of perfectly poached salmon, "another pathetic, jilted American woman seeks my help in tracking down her philandering husband who has no doubt run off with the governess and the family trust account and was last seen swilling gin in Southwark!"

He as much as tossed the letter onto my plate, sat back crossed his arms and scowled. "A junior constable or even a brainless newspaper reporter could find her husband for her. Who in the deuce gave her my name? And she condescends to having her employee write the letter for her."

The letter was typed and bore the letterhead of the Dorchester Hotel on Park Lane. The lady may have been estranged but was clearly not without means.

The Dorchester

Park Lane, Mayfair, London

August 2, 1902.

Dear Mr. Holmes:

I am informed that you are currently in London and are normally to be found in your rooms during the morning hours. Therefore I will call on you at 8:00 am tomorrow.

My employer and I require your assistance in locating her estranged husband who is believed to be living in London. Your services have been highly recommended.

Yours very truly,

Hataniah O'Donnell (Miss)

"The impertinence, do you not agree Watson? How utterly presumptuous. Some Irish spinster who has come back to Britain thinks she can just walk in at any uncivilized morning hour and demand my services."

"Well now Holmes, she is an American after all. You cannot expect the same manners and deference that our English spinsters would exhibit. But we still have a good twenty minutes before she arrives so enjoy some nourishment and brace yourself. I am sure that you will be able to summon your gracious composure and send her on her way within a matter of a few seconds."

We quickly concluded our breakfast and Mrs. Hudson cleared away the dishes. Holmes removed himself from the table to his armchair and lit up his beloved pipe. At 7:50 am the bell rang.

"Confound it!" Holmes shouted, "She has even come early! Mrs. Hudson, you can just leave her standing out there in the rain until the hour strikes."

"I shall do nothing of the kind, Mr. Holmes. She may wait in the hallway if you insist but it is miserable weather outside and I shall bid her enter."

For a moment I thought he would fly into a rage, but he took another draw on his pipe, cocked his head to the side and said, "Well then." He had the faintest trace of a smile on his lips. "If I must be so treated, let us then at least redeem the time by making sport with her. A game of wits, Watson. Are you up for it? Mrs. Hudson shall bring her card and tell us three pertinent facts describing her. You and I, Watson, shall deduce three more facts each about her and we shall see who deduces more of them correctly. If the morning is to start by being wasted then we may as well put our wits to work. What say, Watson, are you ready?" He had stopped slouching into his armchair, was sitting up straight and rubbing his hands together.

"Oh, very well Holmes, if you must. But not one hint of disrespect to the lady."

"Of course not. When have I ever shown disrespect to a lady?"

I thought it better not to answer that. "Please, Mrs. Hudson, let the poor soul in before she catches her death of cold and then bring us her card."

Mrs. Hudson gave us a sideways glance, sighed, and proceeded out the door and down the stairs. A few moments later she re-appeared with just the faintest hint of a sly smile on her face and presented a white calling card to Holmes. I came and stood behind his chair and together we perused it.

Hataniah Mary O'Donnell

Head Foreman - Domestic Affairs

Beulah Plantations
Fayette County, Georgia

"Very well then, Mrs. Hudson. Three facts about her."

"She is American."

"Oh, come, come, Mrs. Hudson, we already knew that."

"That is true Mr. Holmes. But it is also true that she is, you might say, *very* American."

"Yes, go on."

"She is very well dressed in a fine black satiny dress with a full skirt, a black quilted jacket held together by a platinum clasp chain, and has a hat such as an American woman of a certain age might wear to church."

"Indeed. And one last piece of data."

"She is not young, and she is most certainly not starving. There's two for you sir. Now get on with your game. I will not be rude to any guest on my property just so you two layabouts can amuse yourselves."

"You go first, Watson," said Holmes, ignoring our landlady's rebuke. His look spoke volumes as if to say that he had already discerned the poor lady's entire life story.

"By her name, she is Irish," I said.

"Watson," Holmes said with a strong tone of impatience, "I had already deduced that from her letter when it arrived last evening. Surely you can do better than that."

"Fine, if you must," I muttered. I was not at all comfortable with the rudeness we were showing to a guest, even if she was American, by making sport about her while she stood waiting. "She is from County Tipperary." I was not entirely sure of this but had treated some Irish folks by the same name who claimed to have come from there. But of course, with the Irish, you can never be sure. "She left Ireland as a young lass during the great famine some forty years ago, and if it were not for the current situation regarding her employer's husband, she would have never returned, having found much better life on the other side of the pond. There. Is that good enough? Now please, Holmes, get on with your deductions, get this silliness over, and display better manners to your client, even if you are going to decline your services."

Holmes took a deliberately slow inhalation from his pipe and then blew it out even more slowly. He could at times be exceptionally exasperating. I looked over at Mrs. Hudson expecting her to be glaring at Holmes but she was standing serenely in front of the door frame not looking at all vexed as I expected her to, but indeed somewhat smug.

"Not bad at all Watson, although at least half the population of America who have Irish surnames fled the sodden island during the famine. And yes, I do believe that the O'Donnells were from the south of the country. So solidly not bad. Let me add just a few more details. This woman, Miss Hataniah, was the daughter of a professor at Trinity College, Dublin, entered a convent as a teenager, displayed a spirit too contrary for the nuns, was expelled, most likely there was a young man involved, took the women's business diploma at the Alexandra Girls School, had a fight with her family, got on the boat to America, attached herself to a bank in Atlanta, where she met her employer's husband and entered his business as a typist, eventually working her way up through the ranks to the high responsibility she now enjoys."

"And how, dear Holmes, did you come to those conclusions?"

"Elementary. I shall explain them over lunch but first let us see just how right I have been, and then graciously dispose of our impertinent American. Mrs. Hudson, will you please," he said gesturing that she show our guest in.

Mrs. Hudson departed and we heard her ask our guest to ascend the stairs. The sound of the footfalls on the stairs was telling. They were slow. The first ten stairs were climbed and then the sounds stopped.

"Ah yes," said Holmes, "She is truly old and heavy."

Then the next four stairs. Then another rest. Then the final three.

Mrs. Hudson turned to Holmes and I and with a face straining to be straight, announced, "Mr. Holmes, Dr. Watson, Miss Hataniah O'Donnell."

The woman who entered the room was not tall, perhaps no more than five feet, but she was indeed large. I estimated close to thirteen stone. Her bosom could only be described as excessively ample. Her dress, jacket and clasps were exactly as Mrs. Hudson had described. She was elderly and her hair was grey and woven into braids that were neatly coiled around the top of her head and sat nearly covered by the black felt hat that would have been stylish in London a decade ago.

Holmes stood starring at her, uncharacteristically speechless, and exuded an air of being completely discomfited. The woman standing before him was anything but what he had deduced. She was a very dark-skinned negress. Her face was deeply lined and of the consistent colour of a fine Belgian chocolate.

Mrs. Hudson gave me a quick look and just a hint of a smile. I returned her look with a small nod and likewise a barely perceptible hint of a smile. As unspoken co-conspirators we both took a secret delight in seeing our truly genius but occasionally pompous friend nonplussed and we knew that we would be giggling about this morning for many months to come as we chortled behind the back of the great detective.

Sherlock Holmes recovered his composure quickly, gave a very slight bow towards Miss O'Donnell and began his well-practiced *Thank you for your interest in us but our specialty really is not appropriate to the problems with which you are dealing but please let me recommend one of my esteemed fellow detectives* . . . but he never even got the first words out of his mouth before Miss O'Donnell had marched fully into the room, passed under Holmes's nose, and dropped her body with a resounding thud into Holmes's armchair.

"Yessums, dem sevteen stairs is mo lac seven hunred when you is seventa seven years ole. Don't just be standin looking hangdog boys. Set yourselves down. Ah ain't goin nowheres for uh few minutes. An pardon me ma'am could you be so kine as tuh bring an ole lady a cup ah hot tea. An ah doan s'pose you got enthin so civ'lized as burbin in this here place but a teensy bit ah Irish whiskey tuh cools it down would be 'preciated. Thank you much, ma'am."

Mrs. Hudson was positively beaming at her and replied, "Of course Miss O'Donnell. You just stay where you are. There's a pot on the stove waiting for you. And I do believe we have some excellent Irish holy water in the cabinet." With that she departed.

Again Holmes started to say something but the formidable presence in the room cut him off and firmly stated, "Ah tole you boys tuh set yorsells down. Maize well. Once a lady sets hersell down it be alright for duh gentlemen tuh do so. Dint yo mommas never teaches you dat. So set down ah said. Wes got some talkin' tuh do for I gets. But there's no bizniss afor ah finishes mah tea. Whah thank you ma'am. That do look like a purfict cup uh tea. Much obliged."

With that she took a long slow sip from the tea cup, closed her eyes and smiled. "Now yous knows it ain't quite as good as burbin but ah fine cup ah tea with somethin' to fort'fy it is all thuh proofs ah needs dat dare be a good gawd up dare in heav'n an he truly done loves His chillrin."

"We do welcome you," I began, "not only to our home but to our fair town of London. It must be quite a strange place to you. Many visitors coming here for the first time do find it rather overwhelming." That was as far as I made it into my well-practiced welcome speech.

"Y'all call dis ah fair city!? *Fair.* London's uh horr'ble place. Why t'ain't dun nutin' but rain cats and dogs since we arrive an when it don't be rainin' it be foggin' and smellin' like somethin' half way 'tween a gator swamp an a cow fart. Y'all got some pretty shops but yous gots yosells some powerful nasty weathah and we already learnt some powerful nasty folks here. So soonah we dun our bizniss and git back to Ayatlanta happyer we be."

I was moved by a wounding of my civic pride to respond but Miss O'Donnell held up her hand and said "Shush. You boys just pipe down till ah finishes mah tea, then we talks." She said this with an air of someone who was used to giving orders and so I and, to my surprise, Holmes both meekly obeyed. For the next two minutes nothing was said and we watched her serenely sipping her tea and looking not only around the room but giving us a good once over looking as well.

"Vair well boys. Yous hired."

With this Holmes jerked his head up and coughed on his pipe smoke. "I beg your pardon madam, I have no idea as to how you go about conducting yourselves in *Ayaatlanta* but that is just not the way we do business here in England. You know nothing at all about my colleague Dr. Watson nor I and we know nothing about you or your so-called *employer.* Both of those pieces of information must be discerned before we will engage our services."

Miss O'Donnell just smiled back at Holmes. It was not only a friendly smile, it was positively condescending. "Mah employer is out in her carriage an ah go an fetch her now an y'all can meet her an lissen tuh her story. An y'all will want then tuh be of use tuh her. Mark mah words on dat one. As tuh what ah needs to know 'bout you boys, ah already knows 'nuff. So yous hired."

"I regret to inform you, madam," Holmes responded with controlled indignation, "I cannot see how you could possibly know sufficient about us. I may have some modest reputation here in London, but I am quite sure that no one in *Ayaaatlanta* has ever heard of me and it is not likely that they ever shall. And pray tell why your employer would send her *foreman* instead of presenting herself to us if she indeed is to be our client?"

"Oh mah dear boy," she said, "she be a vair busy lady an she have tuh sen off tel'grams and letters an do corrs'pondance an she knows, cuz she knows me all her life, dat ah will know who tuh truss and who not tuh. An I truss you boys so yous hired."

"Then pray tell me just what it is that you think you know about us madam since you have not asked us a single question and we have revealed nothing about ourselves to you."

With this she rolled her head back and laughed heartily. "Doan you knows, you doan have tuh be aksin' questi'ns all time. You can learn all yuh needs tuh know jus by lookin' round at lil thins. Dem lil thins dey tell you all yuh needs tuh know bout some un."

The irony of the situation was delightful, or I should say that it was to Mrs. Hudson and me. It was all we could do not to join in her laughter. Holmes's face slowly softened and his intense innate curiosity took control.

"You are, madam, absolutely correct. But please tell me just what it was that you observed that led you to such a friendly conclusion about we two gentleman on whom you had never set eyes until a few minutes ago. I assume that someone recommended us to you? The bobbies? Scotland Yard? Who?"

Again she laughed. "No mah boy. Ah din ask no poeleese, I just took mahself down to duh kitchen of duh hotel an ah aks duh cooks an duh help. An dey say dat famuz 'tective Mistah Shurlack Holmes br duh bess in duh bizness. So we comed here. An ah sees right way dat whah dem folks says is c'rect so I hires you."

"And how did you see that they were correct?" pressed Holmes.

Miss O'Donnell furrowed her brow and stared briefly at Holmes. "If yuh mus know suh, it go like dis. When I was waitin' ouside your door I sees two pair ah men's boots. Right nice they wuz. 'Spensive. But nice shine and well care for. So dat tell me dat the propry'tors ah dis 'tective agency not be poe boys, cuz if you cuddna 'ford decent boots den yous not much a 'tective. But den I sees dat duh boots is two diff'rent sizes an dat sez dare be two boys here not jus' one. Dat gets me won'drin if yous boys is a cupla dem sodomite boys like your wild mistah Oscar dat we hear all 'bout, if yous knows what ah mean."

"I beg your pardon, madam," I interjected, "but Sherlock Holmes and John Watson have never had anything but most honourable of friendships and I . . ."

"Oh now doan yuh go getting' all het up doc. Mrs. Steward, dats mah employah, an ah doan care where some boy wants tuh warm his sausage, if yuh knows whats ah mean. It doan make no never mind tuh us long as he be doin' whats we payin' him for. But I know dat duh minute I walks through yuh door dat y'all ain't dat way incline."

"Indeed, madam" said Holmes, becoming quite intrigued with our guest of a decidedly different hue, "and just how did you discern that?"

"Well suh," she continued, "It cuddna be more obvyus. As soon as ah is in your parlah Doc here give me a quick once ovah an I knows he is one of doz men who knows what a woman look like without no clothes on."

"Madam! I object. How dare you!"

"No 'fence suh, no da lease. You kin say whats you wants but what a gentleman say and what he thinks is two diff'rent things. It be jus dat any man who bin married he knows things that no bach'lor or sod'me boy can, cuz dey doan know. But anah man who is or has bin married he do know. An' uh woman know when a man know. Dat jus sumptin' all women know. An sides dat ah sees dat you got a teensy white mark on yor fourth fingah on yor lef han where you used to has a weddin' ring so dat tell me all ah needs tuh know 'bout you. An as fur you, Mistah Sherlock, ah jus' has to see duh way you lookin' at me an I sees nuttin' at all, meanin' dat you be no moe dan a steer who dun forget what it like to be a bull. So no disrespec' gent'men, dis is jus' whats any woman know.

"And den ah looks 'round your room here an it tells me ever'thin' else ah needs to know."

"Quite remarkable, madam, and just what did you learn about us from examining our abode," asked Holmes.

"Well suh, if you mus know dis room be all neat an clean an all an dat be a good sign, but it for darn sure dat dere ain't no woman livin' here, an dat you ain't no sod'me boys neithah, cuz neithah a woman nor a nice sod'me boy would have so much 'spensive qual'ty furnishin's and have it look so uhgly. You got mor stuff and colours goin' on in here dan ah can shake stick at. Looks like da dawg dun ate duh artist's whole box ah paints and den cum in here and done his vomit.

"No 'fence, ma'am," she said turning to Mrs. Hudson, "Ah knows you mus try powerful hard tuh keep two bach'lors from goin' uhgly but it can't be helped." "Yes, my dear," said Mrs. Hudson, " I do try, but as you know . . ."

"Ah knows. Oh, ah knows. An ah sees that Doc her got his copy uh duh Lancet an he be readin' it so he mus be comp'tent an dil'gent doctor. An you Mistah Sherlock, you got shelves full uh books on chem'cals, an crim'nuls, an you already finish tuhday's newspapah and set it down all mess up like you dun read it right through. So you mus be smart, at lease for uh English mun. An den ah be lookin' at all dees little knick-knack and whatchamacallems all over duh place and dey all been givin' to you by women cuz no man would buy dem for hisself. An' no man give present like dees to othah men.

"Jus look you. Dare be a photo right here buhside where I sittin' an it say 'I shall think of you always' and signed 'I.A.' an on yo' mantel be a snuff box in carved ivorah and ovah dare on de wall be a paintin' of some body's cottage an all flowers all ovah it. Everthin' in dis room says yous boys ben given gifts by happy women but no names is attached. So dat says dat you not only dun yo' job real good othah wise nobody give you nuttin', but dat you done lots ah good jobs for women who was grateful cuz dey need you tuh be real discrete an all.

"An then ah looks at thuh wall," she said pointing to the open expanse of plastered wall on the far side of our parlour, "an' dare is a whole bunch ah patches dat bin painted ovah an' doze patches is in duh shape of thuh letters 'V' an' 'R'. An' dat sez tuh me dat some damn fool bin doin' his revolver shootin' practice here in duh parlah. So yous may be powerful strange but one ah yous, an I 'spectin' it be you Sherlock, is one vair good shot. An dat be a good thin' if wes needin' protecshun. So what else do ah need? Now if y'all 'scuse me ah go back down your stairs an fetches mah employah."

"Truly remarkable. Absolutely remarkable!" gushed Holmes looking as if he had just met his *doppelganger.* "But please, madam, permit me one more question before we move on to the concerns of your employer. Why did she not just come into our rooms directly herself? It would have saved her considerable time and you could still have imparted all of your remarkable discernments to her?"

"O, she be a vair smart women, suh. An she hate tuh wase time. So she sens me up here firs' tuh souce out yous boys an den go an tell 'er if you be like all doze othah English boys we met, you knows, all doze whos air'gant, 'noxious, self-'fatuated fools an' stupid tuh boot, or if yous be othahwise. So now ah knows an I go gets my employah."

With this she placed her two hands firmly on the arms of Holmes's chair, leaned her large body forward and with an effort raised herself and found her balance on her feet. She started walking slowly towards the door.

I rose to my feet. "May I assume, Miss O'Donnell, that you have concluded that we are *not* like the rest of the English boys. We thank you for the compliment," I said as she shuffled towards Mrs. Hudson, who was offering her arm to assist her down the stairs.

"I kin only say for shuh dat y'all ain't stupid. Duh res' ull have tuh wait. An you maise well stop callin' me Miss O'Donnell. Wes 'mericans and doan stan on silly pompis formal'ty. Ah be callin' you 'Doc' and you 'Sherlock' and if ah gits to likin' you it be 'Sher-boy' so y'all maise well be callin' me 'Momma' cuz dats all an'body dun call me for goin' on sixtah years." And with that she slowly descended the stairs.

CHAPTER TWO - STARLET

"It is sad that I must stand on my principles and decline to take a case that is about nothing more than chasing American husbands," said Holmes with a sigh, "as it would be a thoroughly enjoyable diversion to work alongside such a remarkable woman. Yes. Delightful.

"Hmm. And what have we here?" he continued, as we peered down into the street from our bay window. "Our Momma is leaning into a very well-polished carriage with as fine a uniformed driver and brace of horses as we ever see on Baker Street. I believe that is the coat of arms of Knightsbridge Livery on the door, is it not Watson?"

"Yes indeed it is," I said. "Oh. Look, Holmes, there is a third member of the entourage." We observed first Momma, followed by a tall gentleman in a morning suit, and then by a lady covered in a forest green cloak, completed by an ermine fringed hood covering her head. They entered our door and we heard the group of them ascending our stairs.

Mrs. Hudson opened the door and the first to enter it was a very tall young man, truly no more than a youth. He could not have been much beyond seventeen years old. The most striking thing about him was his height. Sherlock Holmes himself is tall and lean, somewhat over six feet, but this young gentleman had half a foot on Holmes, which, thanks to years of being so lectured by Holmes, I immediately discerned were partly due to the heels of his boots. The boots were a military issue and of fine quality with noticeable wear on the instep section and up the side of the foot, clearly indicating some hard use in a stirrup. He had jet black hair, and except for his broad mouth, strong aquiline features, although his ears seemed a little overly large for such a handsome face. His shoulders were already broad and even with a morning jacket and waistcoat it was obvious that there was not an excess ounce of fat on his powerful young body.

He was carrying a rather large portmanteau, which he immediately placed on the floor just inside the door and in a couple of long strides crossed the floor until he was face to face with Sherlock Holmes. With a gleaming guileless smile, he held out his hand to Holmes who instinctively accepted it.

"Good morning Mister Holmes." he said as he pumped Holmes hand firmly, "It is an honour to meet you. You have many fans and followers in Atlanta. I am Reginald Steward, but everyone calls me Reggie, so please do. And you," he said, turning to me, "must be Doctor Watson. All of my fellow cadets read every one of your stories in *The Strand.* They will be most envious to know that I have been in your presence." He shook my hand as well and moved back towards the door and stood at ease beside it.

His friendly and humble confidence without a hint of affectation was highly pleasing. He was very young to have acquired such ease and social grace and it spoke of a very admirable job by both his family and his schoolmasters. I could see that Holmes had drawn the same conclusions as I, and wondered what else he had seen in this impressive young gentleman.

As expected Momma climbed the steps much more slowly than our young Adonis. She entered the room huffing and puffing, with a fine bead of sweat now on her furrowed brow. Without a word she walked decidedly across the room and again deposited her heavy frame in Holmes's armchair. Had it been anyone else to have twice so violated his *sanctum sanctorum* Holmes would have had a fit of apoplexy, but he acquiesced with a smile and went so far as to briefly place a warm hand on her shoulder.

Now our attention was turned to the figure standing in our doorway. Had I been given to the vice of profanity I am sure I would have gasped, "oh . . . my . . . God!" for standing in our presence was the most magnificent embodiment of mature female pulchritude that I had even gazed upon. She had a striking and queenly appearance, holding herself not just confidently but regally. The four inch heels on her over-the-calf laced-up boots added to her natural stature, making her as tall as Holmes. Her rich black hair, streaked with strands of silver, fell from the crown of her head to her shoulders. The faint lines across her high forehead and the small crowsfeet at the edges of her bright emerald eyes added depth to her utterly arresting visage. The upper part of her face bore an unmistakable resemblance to the young man who now stood beside her. Her lower face narrowed into a perfectly rounded V and her mouth, irresistibly accented by perfectly applied lipstick, was a weapon that could disarm any man as it closed into a girlish pout or broadened into a smile.

After removing her cloak and handing it to an attentive Mrs. Hudson, in a manner almost identical to that of the young man's she strode across the floor towards Holmes. Her dress was a rich burgundy velvet. The yoke was just low enough to expose the upper circles of a god-given bosom. Her puffed sleeves covered her arms only to a place just below her shoulders, exposing firmly defined upper arms. What caused me again to come close to gasping out loud was the cut in the side of her dress that extended well above the knee, permitting a flash of her leg and lower thigh with each confident step she took. She offered her hand to Sherlock Holmes who, carefully maintaining his impassive face and composure, accepted it.

"Good morning Mr. Holmes. You really must forgive our intruding on you at this ungodly early morning hour but I am a lady in rather urgent need of your services and time is of the essence."

"Please madam," he gestured towards the settee, "do make yourself comfortable, and I am sure our good Mrs. Hudson can organize a cup of her finest tea. And would you take some toast? It is still very early and I fear you might not have had the time to enjoy breakfast."

"Thank you sir," she said as she lowered her perfectly contoured body onto the cushions, "but we did indeed depart from the hotel at a very early hour and had time to take our breakfast by Marble Arch before coming to see you. Why, good morning, Dr. Watson." she said looking directly at me, "my son is such a devotee of your intriguing stories about our favourite detective. Is that not so, Reggie?"

"Yes mother," replied the tall young gentleman, "I am planning to return to Georgia with as many autographed copies of the latest *Strand* as I can fit into my baggage."

"Now Mr. Holmes," she said, turning to face my esteemed companion, "I do expect that you are about to tell me that my situation is precluded from your services but I assure you that it truly is not and if you will permit me to tell you my story I am sure that you will agree and respond to our request for your assistance."

She did not wait for Holmes to respond as it was quite obvious that he was being given no choice in the matter but that acceding to her demands was not at all against his wilting will.

"My husband, who I must now locate without delay, and I met during those glorious days, now lost to all but memory, immediately prior to the War for the Independence of the South. We became enamored of each other after a fashion during that tragic war, and eventually married after it ended during that time falsely termed by Yankees as our "Reconstruction." Our marriage was passionate but you might say tumultuous. We were blessed with the gift of a beautiful daughter who was killed in a dreadful accident while she was still a child. I conceived a second time but I unfortunately miscarried so our having more children was not to be. My husband chose to live apart from me for sometime thereafter. But I returned to my family's land and restored it hoping that by doing so he would be drawn back to me and indeed he was.

"He stayed briefly, but then he left again, only to return. This pattern repeated itself several times. It was in part a result of both he and I being very strong-willed people and entering into what we both came to regret as furious clashes. But it was also the result of who, in his heart, my husband is as a man. The sedate life of managing a plantation was not his cup of tea." Here she turned to Mrs. Hudson, "And speaking of which I do thank you. This is excellent.

"My husband, Captain Brett Steward, in his heart and soul, is a soldier of fortune. He has an overpowering weakness of believing in lost causes as he would say, 'Once they're really lost.' So for the past thirty years he has been a very highly regarded mercenary consultant to generals, rebels, politicians . . . anyone who was fighting a battle for a cause that Brett would support but which had almost no hope of ever triumphing. He bore no allegiance to any nation except to the now vanquished Confederate States of America, which, Lord willing, will some day rise again but that is another story. Seventeen years ago, during one of his returns to Beulah – the name of our plantation – I, perhaps in desperation, suggested that we take a honeymoon to make up for the one we had never had when we were first married. The place I selected had become recently famous as the honeymoon capital of America. I am speaking of Niagara Falls, the great cataract beside the Canadian border."

"Yes. Yes. We have all heard about this romantic location," said Holmes. "I believe that our Mr. Oscar Wilde, with whom Momma seems familiar, described it as 'the second great disappointment of American married life.' But pray, please continue."

"To my surprise Brett agreed and we spent two very, shall I say, *intense* weeks. We went on delightful tours, stood arm in arm beside the raging waterfall, bought each other some very fine and personal gifts on the Canadian side of the border where all of the British merchants from Toronto have what they call their outlet shops. In the lovely hotel overlooking The Falls we engaged in what I believe you would term *conjugal interludes* that were passionate and pleasurable beyond description. I was kissed, and kissed often by someone who knows how. My husband, even if by then being a man in his early fifties, was still heavily muscled, very athletic, a gifted and generous lover, and wonderfully endowed. I assume you understand what I am saying gentlemen."

"Of course, madam," I came close to shouting. I was aghast at hearing this far too frank allusion to what for decent English people are strictly private matters. I was particularly appalled that a mother would be making such statements in front of her young son, who though manly was still a callow lad many years from marriage. I glanced first at Momma who was all but ignoring her employer and lost in the enjoyment of her second cup of tea which I gathered the generous Mrs. Hudson had thoughtfully adulterated to her taste. I then looked toward Reginald on whose behalf I was deeply concerned knowing that he would be terribly embarrassed if not humiliated by his mother's indiscrete description of his father. To my shock he was still standing comfortably at-ease but fixing his gaze on his mother in a manner that could only be described as *adoring*. The insight to which this led was even more shocking. Both he and

Momma had heard this all before. It was completely old hat. Mrs. Steward had no doubt made these statements about her husband, the boy's father, to him and to anyone else within earshot. Inwardly I groaned and despaired that America would ever become a civilized country. Then on she went . . .

"Sad to say we ended our time together with an enormous row. It was over my demand that he return to Clayton County and to our land. Land, I believed in my heart, was the only thing worth fighting for. I wanted Brett to love our land the way my Irish father did and return and assume his duty as one of the leading landowners in north Georgia. He steadfastly refused to do so insisting that the only way he would ever return would be in a coffin at which time they could elect him a member of our city council. Looking back I have to confess that my motives were not entirely for the good of our fine city. I had grown obsessively fond of his glorious administrations to my body and once again having tasted of the forbidden fruit was not inclined to let it part from me."

'Please, madam, please,' I said to myself. 'If you are not concerned for the sake of your young son and employee at least see that there are ladies present.' Here I was thinking about defending the virtue of Mrs. Hudson. To my dismay she appeared to be hanging on to every word. Her hands were being squeezed together, her lips had been moistened by her tongue, and she was undeniably flushed. Dear God.

"Brett departed directly from Niagara Falls to parts unknown. I returned to Atlanta, seething with a mixture of anger and passion all wound up together but obligated to do my duty as the owner of one of the largest plantations in Georgia. The following months and years were very profitable as we expanded our acreage and cotton production, and our lumber business, and continued to rebuild our fine city. But they were personally painful as I had no idea where my husband was. I heard nothing from him after that honeymoon, and to this day have had no personal communication from him.

"To my surprise I realized that at some point during that passionate time beside The Falls I had conceived. I had believed that given my age and having been told that after my miscarriage I would not be able to have any more children that the chances of my being fertile were non-existent. But here I was in the family way and no idea where on earth my husband and my child's father could be found."

"My dear lady," I said in my most doctorly consoling voice, "I am sure that must have been a very trying time. But be assured that we have dealt with many sensitive family situations that had the potential for scandal and are more than prepared to use the utmost discretion in all of our services to you."

The woman looked at me as if I had just emerged into civilization from the jungles of Borneo. Then she broke out into a pleasant peel of laughter.

"Oh my, oh my, doctor. You have obviously never been to Atlanta. I declare you have never even been to America. Why, after our dreadful war in which so many of our men were lost, for a woman of my age to have a living breathing husband at all and not be widowed was a blessing. To have one who was not all crippled up with war wounds or gone all Tom o' Bedlam in the head was rare. And to have one who was known to be handsome and wealthy and generous, even if not physically present, was to be considered most fortunate indeed.

"And there was no doubt that Reginald was his father's son. All they had to do was look at him and he had Brett written all over him, The spittin' image as we say in Georgia.

"And as for scandal. Fiddle-dee-dee! We are Americans. As Brett once told me, 'With enough courage you can do without a reputation.' It also helps if you are one of the wealthiest women in the city and provide reliable employment to over three thousand people irrespective of their colour and give fair wages and help build the hospital for our veterans. Why then you can ride stark naked down Peachtree Street like your lady Godiva and receive nothing but smiles and reports in the papers about your *charming eccentricities.*"

Holmes said nothing and continued to fix his gaze on this quite unusual woman. Momma continued to sip her tea, and the boy continued to gaze on his mother with unabashed admiration. I could do no more than sputter, "Yes of course madam. Such things would be highly irregular here in England. But I am sure that your husband was thrilled with the prospect of another child, especially a son who has grown up to be such a fine young man. His father must be very proud of him."

Her face fell. I observed the faint trace of a tremble in her lower lip. "No Doctor Watson, his father is not proud of his son. Neither is he un-proud of his son. My son's father does not know that his son even exists."

She paused here. This was an issue of some pain to her and even such a supremely confident woman had to take a moment to recover her emotional equanimity.

"Brett has never returned to Atlanta. I have sent him many letters informing him about Reggie. Whenever I received news of where he might be found I posted yet another letter. I sent them to India, to Russia, to Japan, to Greece, to Serbia, and most recently to South Africa . . . to anywhere and everywhere on earth where there was turmoil and in which a soldier of fortune might be serving a worthy cause.

"Every one of my letters has been returned to me unopened and marked "Whereabouts Unknown." To this day Brett Steward does not know that his son is the pride of the new Georgia Military Academy and the idol of every debutante in the city."

Here I glanced up again at the young man. He was looking down at his boots and blushing. How unusual that a young lad could be so proud of his mother even as she bragged about his father's endowment but then so embarrassed when she bragged about him.

"Permit me to ask the obvious question." Holmes finally said, breaking his silence. "Why now? Why after all these attempts to locate your husband have you taken it upon yourself to come to London to try to track him down in person?"

"In May Reggie graduated from the Georgia Military Academy with exceptionally high honors. He has received acceptance with full scholarship to our most prestigious school in the South, the Military College of South Carolina. We know it by its more familiar name of *The Citadel.* His father also attended *The Citadel,* after being expelled from West Point, and had outstanding accomplishments. He still holds the school's record for many of its military, sporting, and academic contests. Now Brett, being Brett, failed to graduate due to some charges laid against him for some minor misdeeds connected to bringing girls into the dormitories, alcohol consumption, and feeding some sort of nutrients to the faculties' horses causing them to have severe diarrhea during a parade day.

"His writing essays in the school newsletter criticizing in the most severe terms our politicians and the military leadership of our Southern regiments and noting how much more prepared were the regiments in the North, made him very unpopular with some of those in power although looking back he was absolutely correct in his assertions and sadly all too prescient. He now is esteemed by the school and they claim him as one of their own even though they also expelled him so many years ago. His providing funds for their new armory has not hurt.

"But they do have one inviolable rule concerning admissions. The Citadel must act *in loco parentis* and requires all parents of cadets to sign permission forms giving them this unrestricted right. These must be signed by both parents unless one of them is known to be deceased. Since his father is believed by all to be alive it is required that he sign the documents. Forgery is out of the question, not because I would not hesitate to do it but because I am sure it would be found out, bring dishonor to my son, and destroy his opportunity for a brilliant military career.

"The school term begins on the second Monday of September. It is now the third of August. There is little time available to us and so I have left my affairs in the capable hands of my Head Foreman for Agricultural Operations, Sam Magnus, and have come to London to find Brett. I placed advertisements in your newspapers announcing my presence and asking and indeed offering to pay for any pertinent information. I have recently met with three of his closest business associates who confirmed that they had recent communication from him, believed him to be either in London or nearby, but had not personally spoken to him nor could they confirm his whereabouts. Since I told you at the outset of this conversation that time was of the essence, I am now here requesting your services Mr. Holmes."

Sherlock Holmes raised his head and his face took on a puzzled and somewhat pained expression. "Mrs. Steward, I cannot but admire all you have accomplished in your life and in that of your son, and I am honored to be solicited by someone so esteemed as yourself, but my special province is in matters that are not only criminal but require an exercise of logical synthesis. While your concerns have been distressing and your ability to rise above them most inspiring, there is nothing you have told me that in any way involves the breaking of the law. Doing dastardly things to the digestive tracks of horses is the closest you've come, and I'm afraid that even that does not constitute a diabolical crime."

She nodded in agreement. "Now don't you go jerking your chin at me Mr. Holmes. I said a moment ago that I had made contact with three men in London who had some sort of recent transactions with my husband although sight unseen."

"Yes, ma'am," I confirmed, "You did indeed tell us that."

"The names of those three men are: Donald McQuarrie, a banker in Mayfair; Boas De Groot, an importer with an office in the City and a warehouse in the Docklands; and Brendan Fitzsimmons, a solicitor on Bedford Row. Now . . . do you see why I am here?"

Mrs. Hudson uttered a fearful gasp. I could not speak. For a quick second Holmes clasped his hands together as if to start rubbing them and immediately recovered himself and returned to his pressing of his fingertips pose.

The three men she named were the three who in the past few days have been murdered by *the mad garrotters.*

"Your police, your Scotland Yard, and your newspapers are all reporting that these men had no connection to each other and that they just unfortunately were in the wrong place at the wrong time when a murderous gang of thugs came along, garrotted them and robbed them. That silliness is what they are saying, is it not Mr. Holmes?"

"Indeed it is, and as usual they are quite wrong," replied Holmes.

"Yes. There is a connection and it is my husband, Captain Brett Steward. They were all in contact with him during the past year and now they are all dead. So that is why I am here Mr. Holmes. My husband's life is quite likely in danger and I need your help to protect him."

I asked her, "Have you spoken to the police or Scotland Yard, Mrs. Steward?"

"I spoke to them yesterday afternoon as soon as I learned about the third murder. They were very officious and sympathetic and all but made it quite clear that they could not help me look for a husband who would not be found. I do believe that they thought I was just one more American woman searching for some wayward husband who had emptied the family's accounts, run off with the governess and was now hiding out in London. I must confess that I was more than a little disappointed that they could be such obnoxious fools."

I could not resist a glance in the direction of Sherlock Holmes. He had been called many names in his career but never to my memory obliquely referred to as an obnoxious fool. I stole a glance at Mrs. Hudson as well and noticed that she was biting her lower lip. Then we noticed Holmes glaring angrily at both of us so we had to look at the floor and pretend to be inspecting the carpet.

Holmes turned to the woman who had become most assuredly our latest client.

"Mrs. Steward . . ."

"Sir, if we are to be working together to protect my family then I would prefer that you address me as Miss Starlet, which is how I am known to all in Atlanta, indeed it is how all the men of my age, what few there are in Atlanta, address me. Those men and I shared four years of war and it gave us the right to be familiar with each other. I expect that you and I are about to enter some dangerous times and a more informal form of speaking to each other would be quite acceptable."

"Thank you Miss Starlet," said Holmes. Using a client's Christian name took a concentrated exercise of the will on his part. "Leave these matters in our hands. We shall do everything in oun power not only to protect your husband but to bring these murderous thugs to justice. I must however correct one of your misconceptions."

"Yes, and just what might that be?"

"You said that the obvious connecting link between the murders of these three men was some form of communication they had with your husband sometime during the past year or two."

"Yes. Why, what else could it have been? The police know of no other business, family or social connection they had to each other."

"My dear lady. The connection to your husband was only secondary. They all shared a much closer tie in their business dealings. They all had a direct meeting with the same person during the final days before their deaths." Holmes paused, waiting for Miss Starlet to comprehend the gravity of what he had said to her.

She stared at him blankly for a few seconds, and then her eyes widened with a look of fear and shock. "Yes. Of course. Their immediate link with each other was not with Brett. It was with . . . *me.* Those murderers have been following me. And Momma. And Reggie. And now all three men are dead. Most horribly murdered. I led those villains to those three innocent men."

"Yes, I fear that what you say, Miss Starlet, is indeed what has happened but there is no way you could have known that," said Holmes. "We do not know why they were following you but we must acknowledge that not only is your husband in danger but most probably you, your son, and Momma are as well."

Miss Starlet retained her regal posture and demeanor but I noticed that she was squeezing her right hand and pressing her thumbnail into the section of her index finger that is just behind the first knuckle. "Gentlemen," she said in a deliberate tone, "I have been through many difficult times in my life. I do not fear for myself, nor to lie, steal, cheat or kill if I were forced to. However three innocent men have already died for no other reason than their contact with me. The two people who are nearest and dearest to me on this earth are sitting in the room. Their lives may be in grave danger and it would be because of my actions. I do not blush to admit that I am quite frightened and I place myself in your hands seeking your guidance for our safety."

Holmes had been drawn into one the roles that had made him such a great detective. He would assume his destined place as the protector of the fairer sex and would leave no stone unturned, no enemy unvanquished until his charges were restored to safety. "Miss Starlet," he said, "you may trust in our devotion to your needs and those of your family. But know I must ask that you reveal to me all that you have learned about your husband's activities since your arrival here in London. As you said, 'Time is of the essence.'"

She nodded. "We arrived in London ten days ago. I had received some pieces of correspondence from London regarding transfers of funds and properties from Brett's affairs but had heard nothing at all for the several months. Since these were my only sources of information I began with them."

"Entirely sensible," I said with an affirming nod hoping to diminish some of the intense feelings she had concerning her role in the death of these three gentlemen by such nefarious means.

"All three of them acknowledged that they had had some contact with Brett in the past and that, following his explicit instructions, they had forwarded various transactions over to me. But they also were quite certain that they had never been informed of his address here in London, and that they had heard not a peep from him in-person in over two years. I suspected that all three of them were withholding some information from me but they would say no more than what I have just told you.

"I requested that they turn over to me whatever papers or other records they possessed, which they did."

"Indeed?" queried Holmes, "with no objection?"

"The objections were dealt with. Before his departure from America Brett had left fully signed and sealed documents giving me power of attorney over his affairs in the event he could not be located. I merely had to produce these and such records as they held were given to me. They are all in the valise that my son has brought with us. You may look over everything," she said.

"We shall examine all of the contents very carefully, you may be sure," said Holmes. "Our first priority though is your safety. You may assume that you will be followed unless we take evasive precautions."

"We are grateful for your concern. We departed the hotel at such an early hour this morning that I am sure that no one has followed us here."

"I am certain as well," said Holmes, "We have seen no one looking up from Baker Street and had they sought to conceal themselves we would have had a report from our splendid company of Irregulars."

"Who dey?" said Momma, who had long since lost interest in her fortified tea and been following every word of the conversation since the issue of danger to her charges had been voiced.

"*Dey,*" said Sherlock Holmes, with a warm smile towards Momma, "are the best troop of spies in the city and I am sure that when you meet them they will endear themselves to you as much as they have to me. You may also be sure," he said turning back to Miss Starlet, "that our adversaries will be watching your hotel and on seeing you return will immediately realize that they missed you this morning on account of your early departure and that they will not make that mistake again tomorrow.

"So please follow these instructions to the letter," said Holmes. "I shall send a note to Master Toby St. John, the head doorman of the Dorchester. He is a stalwart yeoman and regards the safety of his guests as a divine trust. I will ask him to furnish young Reginald with a cab driver's uniform such as would be used for drivers attending at the door of the Dorchester. I'm sure that he can come up with one large enough. Some of our drivers are as tall as your son and you will just have to cinch in the belt and trousers. With a good top hat that should be enough to get past their enemy's lookouts. As for you my dear lady . . ." he paused here, touching his fingertips together, "the most reliable disguise would be to have you dressed as a man."

"Whoa dare Sherlock!" said Momma. "Dat jus tain't fittin'."

"And just what do you mean, my dear Momma by *'tain't fittin'?*"

Momma lowered her head and glowered back at him. "If sumtin' ain't fittin' it jus' 'tain't fittin'. An' wha' you suggestin' jus' 'tain't fittin'. Das all."

Holmes looked over at Miss Starlet who gave a nod of acquiescence towards Momma and then looked back at Holmes with an expression that said, *and just what might be your next best suggestion?*

Holmes looked intently at Miss Starlet. I could tell that he was redrawing her striking figure in his mind and seeking to imagine what possible disguise could conceal her identity. His smile indicated that he had decided on an alternative. He raised himself from his chair and retired briefly to his rooms. He returned bearing in his hand a mane of flowing red hair. "Then Madam you will have to wear this wig and I am sure you have an evening gown with you, one that could be described, shall we say as *daring*. As you depart the hotel just before the breakfast hour please have your red hair in a somewhat disorderly fashion. You may attend to your rouge and lipstick in the cab."

"Mistah Holmes!" Momma burst out, "I nevah but once seen hair dat cullah in mah whole life. Ever'bodah dat see dat and her flauntin' her buzzim 'fore three 'clock in thuh aftahnoon think she no more dan white trash, uh high-priced woman uh ill ree-pute!"

"Thank you Momma. That is exactly what they need to think. Could you play such a role convincingly, Miss Starlet?"

"I could have danced with Abe Lincoln if I'd had to, so I am quite sure I could do what you ask," she responded with a sly smile. "I have just the dress in mind; the one Brett made me wear years ago when he was demanding the same theatrical effect. With my young and handsome driver the most observant of spies shall be thoroughly fooled."

Dear me, can this woman honestly be pleased to dress up like a prostitute and have her son drive her through London? My question was being answered in the affirmative. Merciful heavens. These Americans.

Holmes now turned towards Momma. "And you my dear lady, I shall have to ask to remain at the hotel but making yourself visible from time to time in the lobby and the dining room so that our spies will believe your entire party is still in the building."

"Ah kin do dat," she answered, still frowning at Holmes and Miss Starlet. "Ah cud even have da dinin' room sen' up lunches for four jus' to fool dem suh more."

"Splendid," exclaimed Holmes, "I am quite sure that you missed your divine calling as a detective."

"No suh. Duh good Lord dun call me tuh be a honest Christian woman."

Holmes was struggling for a rejoinder but admitted defeat and simply rose from his chair, offered his hand to Momma and said, "Then allow me to assist an honest Christian woman to her carriage. I shall see you two tomorrow morning at the same time by our front door. And please, young soldier, leave the valise where it is. By tomorrow morning we will have gleaned all there is to learn from it."

Mrs. Hudson interposed herself and took Momma's arm and helped her down the stairs. Miss Starlet and Reggie followed. From the window we watched them drive off towards Hyde Park.

CHAPTER THREE - BRIANY

Sherlock Holmes's complexion had visibly altered as it always did when his animal spirits were enlivened and he was engaged in hot pursuit of the latest evil doers. He moved with deliberate energy as he made notes and plotted out his route to the undoing of his now doomed adversaries.

Holmes reached for the valise and laid it on our table. He opened the latches and looked inside without saying anything. It contained three distinct bundles, each tied up with a ribbon to which a note was attached identifying its origins.

He turned to me. "We have entered a very dangerous game, my dear friend. It is not only afoot, it is running very quickly and we shall have to make haste to get in front of it. Otherwise our lovely client's husband's life will most certainly be shortened, as may be hers. We are dealing with very dangerous killers and there is no time to waste. I shall first organize the Baker Street Irregulars to bring us every shred of information available about a small band of garrotters and then make visits to the offices of the recently deceased.

“I shall need your assistance. I do not have adequate time left in the day to investigate all the data pertaining to the murders of these three unfortunate men and at the same time thoroughly examine the contents of this valise. So my dear man if I may prevail upon your good graces and ask if you would be so kind as to review these papers while I haste myself about London. I ask only that you would seek in them the data that I would were I perusing them. Of all people you are the most familiar with my methods. May I beseech you accordingly, my good doctor?"

"Of course you may," I assented, "but I fear I shall disappoint you yet again as no matter how many times I have observed you at work I have never fathomed the methods you employ to see details that are so obvious to you and missing to my dull eye. But I shall do my best and have the best report I can muster for you upon your return."

"I could ask no more, my dear friend," and with this he departed the rooms and descended the stairs. I heard his bird whistle sound and from the window could see the ragamuffins he so endearingly termed his Company of Irregulars assemble around him for a minute. Then he leapt into a cab which forthwith began to move at breakneck speed south on Baker Street and towards the City.

My day's task, long and exacting, was laid out in front of me. I trust that my dear readers will bear with me as I plod my way through the details of my discoveries.

I first rang for a cup of tea which the peerless Mrs. Hudson delivered to my desk and then I began to sort and sub-divide. The first group of documents all concerned shipments from various parts of the globe which arrived at the Port of London and were handled by the agent, the late Mr. de Groot. The bills of lading and way bills all noted the ports of origin - Singapore, Colombo, Rangoon, Tokyo Bay, Calcutta (several times), Vancouver, San Francisco, Rio De Janeiro, St. Petersberg . . . almost every major port on earth. The names of the ships were duly listed and all documents were appropriately signed and sealed. What was unusual was that in the entry for the size of the shipment many were marked a "Grade 1", the smallest, no more than a cigar box. Yet every one of them was also accompanied by a certificate of insurance from Lloyd's and the rating of every certificate stated "Maximum £10,000." The "Protection" entry was invariably marked "Grade 10" - the ship's safe in the captain's quarters. Scribbled on the way bills were some markings in pencil with letters like "D" or "R" or "E" or occasionally "Au" or "Ag."

I did not have to be Sherlock Holmes to deduce that our wayward husband, Captain. Steward, had been sending back packets of gold, silver, diamonds and precious gems from the various corners of the earth in which he sought his fortune, and a considerable fortune it was indeed.

Within two hours I had completely sorted the shipping documents and arranged them chronologically. Over the past fifteen years our man had roamed the earth. From my memory it appeared that each of his temporary sojourns corresponded with some type of conflict. He had been in Burma when the Burmans were giving the BEF a bad case of the Irrawaddy chills; in Shanghai while the Chinese and the Japs were having a go at each other; in western Canada while thousands of men "crazed for the muck called gold" were trekking their way to the frozen hills of the Yukon; in the Dominican when Teddy Roosevelt and his silly Roughriders were storming San Juan Hill . . . and so it went. It began in Paris with the uprising of the Commune and had ended just over two years ago in Pretoria. After that, nothing.

Interspersed with the highly valued and insured shipments were some rather curious ones. Every year without fail in early August and again in early December there were copies of shipping documents for articles sent to Calcutta. These were handled by a different agent who

I gathered was a correspondent office for Mr. De Groot, and were all marked "D.G.H." They were not large items in size and had no insurance certificates. They took place like clockwork during the early years but then came to an end eight years ago. For these I could deduce no reason at all.

Holmes had often observed that you could tell as much about a man from his bank book as you could from his diary and so I duly studied the details of Captain Steward's financial transactions. Since 1864 he had maintained an account at a bank in Liverpool. At one point late in 1866 the balance had surged to over one million pounds. Beginning in the 1870s there were large deposits exceeding a thousand pounds on an irregular basis that I cross-referenced with the shipments of gold and gems. Every quarter during the early years he sent £3000 to the account of the Beulah Plantation in Atlanta. Later this increased to £4000 and then £5000. Irregular payments were recorded to several firms that included Beretta, Colt, Remington and Rolls-Royce. There were miscellaneous payments to accounts at Harrod's, Fortnum and Mason's and several of London's better haberdashers, and some smaller sums were sent to a Barings branch in Calcutta but these had also been curtailed eight years ago. Then starting a little less than eight years ago transfers to an *O'Brien Trust* appeared and continued quarterly up until the latest recorded statement of the immediate past month. The cash balance was consistently maintained at just over £20,000 and when it exceeded that amount there were transfers to Hitchens, Harrison and Co. who I knew to be one of the major brokerages on the London Exchange. I assumed that our man was purchasing securities and wisely not leaving his funds in unproductive cash. Our Captain Steward was a very wealthy man and an astute manager of his financial affairs.

Throughout the records various transactions had been initialed. Prior to 1898 they were clearly signed as 'RB" which I concluded were those of Brett Steward, our wayward husband. Thereafter a different set of initials appeared. In what was clearly a female hand were the initials 'BO.' Given the impressive size of the transactions this Miss or Mrs. BO must be a woman of competence in whom our man placed great trust. Suspicions concerning our man's fidelity crept into my mind and I feared that the heart of our magnificent client might again be broken. But *honi soit qui mal y pense* and so these thoughts I had to banish from my mind as I turned to the thick file of documents that had come from his solicitor.

Most of what I found in the now deceased solicitor's file was received correspondence related to various business transactions. Many of these letters could be referenced back to shipping and financial entries and none seemed unusual given Captain Steward's dealings in arms and shipments throughout the globe. There were two sets of personal correspondence that I set aside. The first were of incoming notes bearing the letterhead of *St. Andrew's Mission.* Prior to 1890 the location of the mission was given as Calcutta. Thereafter it read *Kalimpong, Bengal.* The notes were addressed consistently to "My dear Brett" and signed various as "John" or "Rev. John" or "Dr. J" and during the later years of 1892 to 1894 as "Daddy G". The contents were very brief. Some contained a note of thanks for a contribution received related to the construction of a library or dormitory. Others referred to the progress of "B". "B still reserved after loss but bearing up well" read one of the early messages. "B took first in maths" read another dated early on. Most of the later ones likewise referred to the remarkable accomplishments of this young student who was only identified as "B". The last note, dated in 1895 was a little longer and informed Brett that B had graduated and on Prize Day walked away with several academic first prizes as well as ribbons for swimming, athletics and riding. Whoever this young B might be, he was most assuredly an outstanding student. No more notes were received following the graduation notice, except for the odd one again thanking Brett for his monetary contribution to the Scholars' Fund.

The second set of notes bore the handwriting of two different men and were an exchange of quickly dashed off correspondence between them. They had used the same sheet of writing paper both to send the original note and upon which to scribble the hasty reply. Those originating from 'R" bore no letterhead at all prior to 1893 but were on the finest quality linen paper. From 1893 until 1898 they changed and were on paper supplied by Brown's Hotel in Mayfair. After that date they were once again on the same blank pages. Those initiated by the other man, signing as "AE" were embossed with a coat of arms that I recognised but to which I could not immediately attach a name, my memory of English heraldry having faded since my school days. The cryptic messages all appeared to concern the activities and movements of someone referred to as *The BH.* In response to a note from R stating "BH present in the Khyber" AE had replied "Yes and arming the Boxers." From a location identified only as "Sand." was a request from AE, "Is BH in BEG" the reply came back from R "Many as well as on the Venz. Side.", and to which a third note was added "They are leading us to war with the Yanks." Others were in a similar vein except for one from Paris where B had written "Tiger confirms MB was behind Commune."

These and all other papers I laid out neatly in separate piles according to the subject matters and chronologically ordered for Holmes to peruse upon his return. I postponed asking Mrs. Hudson to send in supper and waited for Holmes to return, which he did shortly after six o'clock. He looked tired and hungry but bearing that look of determined satisfaction I had come to know when he was hot on the trail of a worthy adversary. He sat down at our table and poured himself a glass of brandy. Mrs. Hudson appeared soon bearing one of her unfailingly appetizing platters; this one of roast duck.

"Thanks awfully, Mrs. Watson," I said to the good woman.

As soon as we had finished eating I proudly displayed my work and offered some of my insights. Holmes listened politely and said little except the odd murmur of "Yes indeed." Or "Yes. Well done Watson." As his praise was always highly economical I felt quite pleased with my accomplishments. He took my notes and the files in hand.

"Please do not disturb me for the next fifty minutes, Watson. This will be a three pipe review of the data."

Following supper and into the early evening Holmes said not another word but merely smoked his pipe and looked over my various piles of documents, examining some quite closely with his glass.

Precisely fifty minutes later he put down the last letter, stood up, proceeded to the corner of the room and retrieved his violin. He tuned it briefly and began to play one of his familiar favourites by Brahams. This was unbearable.

"Really Holmes," I remonstrated, "you must say something. What have you deduced from your day and from my hours of work."

"Oh, yes, of course, my dear Watson. How thoughtless of me. First thing tomorrow morning we shall reunite our client with her husband and take steps to protect them for they are in great danger from the most ruthless of villains." With that said he placed his bow once more upon the instrument and returned to Brahams. I knew better than to expect anything more from him until morning.

I rose early but Holmes was already up and out of 221B Baker Street. From the window I watched him as he stood at the corner of Portman Close chatting with a troop of his Irregulars. With a wave from the detective his spies scampered off and he returned to his door and came up the stairs.

He sat down to breakfast, tucked in heartily to the kippers and toast that Mrs. Hudson had laid out and engrossed himself in *The Times.*

At 7:55 I heard a carriage on the street below our window and looked down upon a very finely appointed Hanson cab, with a tall driver strikingly attired in a navy blue uniform with flashing gold braids, buttons, epaulettes, and top hat. He descended from his perch at the back of the vehicle, opened an umbrella to offer protection from the rain, unlatched the door, and offered his free hand to his passenger. She stepped out onto the pavement and I inwardly groaned at what our neighbours would think about our latest client. For there emerged from the cab a tall woman with shoulders and arms uncovered in the early morning, a dress with cleavage cut so low as to give a clergyman heart failure, and a mane of red hair such as would be unknown outside of County Cork.

Our clients ascended the stairs and we could hear them laughing and giggling about their disguises. "Oh my, would not Belle have been proud of me? Do you think she would have hired me Reggie?"

"Only if she wanted to take the best clients away from all the other girls. Mother, you look utterly irresistible!"

They continued on in their rather vulgar repartee as they entered the room and proceeded to inform Holmes and me of their triumph in leaving the hotel not only undetected but with glaring stares from the breakfasting patrons and a wink from Toby the doorman.

"Mr. Holmes, Mr. Holmes" began Miss Starlet, "How can I thank you? Knowing that you agreed to protect us so lightened my heart that we did not spend the afternoon in our hotel. I know that it was a little bit risky, but I told our driver to go directly to Harrod's.

"I just had to see what the latest fashions are for the Fall in London so we stopped by the ladies' department and, well, my goodness, they had so many beautiful things to look at."

"Oh my. I introduced myself to the head shoplady and said I was sorry that I had so little cash with me otherwise I would love to buy my entire fall and winter wardrobes from her. And didn't she just give me and odd look and say, 'Madam, we do not need cash. You could just put everything on your husband's account.'

"My darling husband it seems has had an account with them for going on thirty years and has bought many beautiful fashions for women during that time. Well, Mr. Holmes, even if you would not be proud of me, I am sure that your dear Mrs. Hudson would," she said with a beaming smile directed towards the good lady, "because by the end of the afternoon I made sure that more damage had been done that account than had been done in the past thirty years. If we all do make it out of this crazy time alive then Reggie, and Momma, and I will all be the best dressed folks on Peach Tree Street."

Holmes smiled warmly, having enjoyed their tale of retail adventure. "As much as it pains me to make the request, I will have to ask you to change from your current costumes into something more appropriate for a morning drive through London."

"Oh, must we really?" replied Miss Starlet, her face drawn into a well-practiced pout. "Very well then, you are such a spoil sport sir. But I have the most beautiful new white summer dress so I shall not complain." With an impish smile she made her way to one of our back rooms. Her tall handsome son followed bearing a carpet bag in which I assumed he carried newer and more acceptable attire.

They returned forthwith looking splendid in fine quality outfits. Miss Starlet looked at Holmes and with feigned seriousness asked, "Kind sir, do tell this now respectable lady what news of her wandering husband?"

"We are off to Mayfair," announced Holmes, "to pay a surprise visit to your husband and," he added, looking at Reggie, "your father."

The gay smiles slowly vanished from the faces of Miss Starlet and Reggie, struck from their mouths as if by some invisible hand.. They exchanged a glance of apprehension between them and then rose and without a word walked towards the door and descended the stairs. Holmes and I followed and once at the curb of Baker Street, I hailed a four-seater, lucky to find one so readily on such a close and rainy day.

As we drove south on Baker Street towards Oxford I made a few remarks about the weather and tried to add some levity to the moment by repeating Momma's appraisal of London but to no avail. Our clients remained stone-faced, which puzzled me as we were about to accomplish the mission that brought them across the pond in the first place.

Holmes, who I have long admitted was a far better judge of the feelings that people are having in the hearts behind their brave masks, reached across the cab and warmly covered Miss Starlet's hand with both of his. "My dear, there is not a doubt in my mind that your husband will find you every bit as attractive as he did in the past. You have only become all the more lovely with the passing of time."

She glanced at him and gave a forced smile. "Four decades have passed since he looked upon me as a pretty and head-strong young girl and told me that I was no lady. That girl doesn't exist anymore. Nothing turned out the way I expected. Nothing. I fear that now that I have become a lady he will no longer see in me that pretty girl that he once desired so passionately."

"No," said Holmes, "he will not, but he will see an exceptional woman who will be his loving partner and helpmeet until death do you part."

"And you, young sir," he continued, turning to Reggie, "are about to meet a father who will be exceedingly proud of his son."

"Thank you Mr. Holmes," Reggie said, "I confess to an inward fear that I would find it very trying if a father who had abandoned me not knowing of my existence were to do the same thing again after becoming aware of it. My lessons in courage failed to cover events like this one."

"I have no son," said Holmes, looking at Reggie directly, "but if I were to suddenly discover that I had one I would give thanks to Providence if he were to be half-way close to who you are. You will be just fine, mark my words."

"Thank you sir," the boy replied, "you are being kind as well as competent."

"May I again ask you" said Miss Starlet, having somewhat recovered her composure, "where it is that we are going?"

"To Mayfair," said Holmes, "your husband has rooms at Claridges. As we enter I must ask you please to follow my lead and play the game with me."

We had driven down Park Lane, turned left into Brook Street, and arrived at the door of the recently restored and re-opened Claridges Hotel, which had once again returned to its status as the most respected and exclusive in all of London. Holmes led the way up the steps, breezed confidently past the attentive doorman, and approached the desk of the porter.

"I bid you good morning sir, my name is Sherlock Holmes." The porter raised his eyebrows while Holmes continued. "Our visit to your most reputable establishment is only for good reasons, I assure you. I am certainly not here to investigate anything untoward. This American lady, Mrs. Smith, is my client. Her son, Theodore, has completed his schooling and is about to engage on his grand tour of our fair land and the Continent. While doing so he will need a continuing place to return to and I have recommended that he take rooms at Claridges."

"Why thank you sir. Our reputation is very dear to us and knowing that our most famous detective attests to our quality is a very kind compliment," the porter replied with a trace of an authentic smile.

"You must understand, however," Holmes said, "that people in the colonies hear only those things about London that the most miserable of our reporters on Fleet Street tell the world, and so they fear that our streets are filled with cutthroats and villains, and our hotels with touts and swindlers. I have brought Mrs. Smith here today to prove to her that her son will be completely safe and secure."

"Of course sir. The blackguards of Fleet Street do the Empire no favours by such inflammatory stories."

"I heartily agree. So may I impose upon your fine hospitality with two requests. Would you be so kind as to show young Theodore here a set of rooms – we have noted that you have several vacancies posted – and may I also, in strictest confidence of course, be permitted to see the list of your continuing residents so that I may assure his mother that they are all of the highest moral character and will be a welcome presence in the forming of his character?"

"We do not normally offer the names of our residents to inquiry, sir, protecting as we do their privacy," the porter said, "but as you have assured me of your treating it in confidence, and as I rather suspect that were I to withhold it then Sherlock Holmes would find another way to obtain the information all the same, I will let you observe our list."

From beneath his porter's desk he withdrew a smaller register and opened it to a marked page and spread it in front of Holmes who gestured to "Mrs. Smith" to join him in looking it over. Holmes smiled at the porter, closed the register and handed it back. "Thank you my good man," he said, "although I am not personally acquainted with all of these august persons I can confirm that not one of them is known in any way other than the most positive to Scotland Yard or our local bobbies. And now, sir, if you will give young Theodore a tour of the available rooms I will, with your permission, show this good lady what an excellent job Mr. Doily Carte has done not only in making Claridges a pearl of fine design but the safest in London from fire or thievery. After I do so I will return to your desk and fetch Theodore."

"By all means. We are very proud of our grand hotel. And please, Master Theodore, let me show you to what I am sure will become your most enjoyable home away from home," said the porter and with that he departed with *Theodore* in tow. As soon as he was out of earshot Holmes beckoned me and Miss Starlet to his side.

"He's not here," said Miss Starlet, "You said he was living here but his name was clearly not on that list. We might as well leave."

"I must ask you, my dear Miss Starlet," said Holmes, ever the teacher, "what did you observe about those names?"

Miss Starlet shrugged her shoulders and responded somewhat quizzically, "Nothing unusual. There were about thirty names, all Lord such-and-such or Earl of so-and so. Almost all striking me as oh-so-English, but certainly no *Brett Steward* was inscribed."

"He most certainly was on the register and is living in room 435," said Holmes. "Let us proceed."

She looked at him with a glance of disbelief but said nothing and followed him up the staircase.

"Are we just going to walk in?" asked Miss Starlet.

"No, my dear, we are not 'just going to walk in' we are going to knock and if no one answers we are going to break in," answered Holmes.

At the door marked 435 we knocked and indeed there was no answer. Holmes procured from his pocket a small case that I had last seen when we burgled the residence of the vile Charles Milverton. It contained his collection of exquisitely designed locksmith's tools and, taking one of them in hand, he quickly picked the lock of what I am sure Claridges had advertised as being the latest in safety and security. We entered a room with high ceilings, floor to ceiling windows opening to a small balcony, very fine quality flooring, and lush velvet draperies. There were several paintings on the walls that seemed to be of the most recent avant-garde style from France. Rather blurred and smudged to my mind but then I was no connoisseur of art.

"Your husband continues to have very fine taste," I observed trying to disguise an inkling that the fine taste we were observing betrayed the hand of a lady of considerable breeding and hardly that of a soldier of fortune.

Miss Starlet said nothing. She walked slowly and aimlessly about. "Either he has found a classy mistress or this is not Brett's place at all." she concluded. It was apparent that she thought the former alternative the most likely and was not in a good humour.

"He does live here, stayed here last night, and will most likely be returning presently. "

"How can you possibly know that?" asked Miss Starlet.

"The tobacco ashes in the ashtray are from the Golden Virginia brand. The maids clean the rooms every day in the late morning and again in the evening and no maid of Claridges would be working here long if she were to leave an ashtray unemptied and unpolished. These ashes were dropped by your husband this morning before he left the premises.

"Before he returns I pray you, Miss Starlet," said Holmes, "would you and Dr. Watson please look into all of the armoires, drawers and closets and see what you can find. I will fetch our young Master Theodore from the front desk."

With that Holmes departed the room.

Miss Starlet and I entered one of the bedrooms and began to investigate the closets. She opened a large armoire and examined some of the clothing that was hanging therein. She lifted out a fine cotton shirt and held it up in front of her. "These are his size but I do not recognize any of them. Nor these suits, nor the coats," she said.

"I do not think it likely that a man of your husband's wealth and activities would still be wearing the same clothes as he did seventeen years ago," I offered.

"I suppose you are right," she said while still looking from top to bottom of the armoire. Then I heard a gasp and watched her fall to her knees. She reached into the floor of the armoire and brought out a set of men's boots. "These are his. These are Brett's. I gave them to him." Her voice trembled slightly with barely disguised intense feeling. She stood up, walked over to the bedside chair and sat down, holding the boots in her lap.

"Really, my dear Miss Starlet, how can you possibly remember a set of old black boots? There must be thousands of that style all over London," I said.

"No. No. I am quite certain. On our belated honeymoon in Niagara Falls I saw the store of a Toronto merchant, a bootmaker. So I put a pair of Brett's favourite shoes in my purse and for an hour excused myself claiming a need to purchase some feminine products. I had the bootmaker make two pairs of the highest quality boots for

Brett using his shoes as the pattern. One set was for summer, one for winter. The Canadians you know are very good at making boots for winter, which our Atlanta cobblers, bless their hearts, simply are not. These are his winter boots. Look, here. Inside."

I looked. "Meyers, Toronto" was printed on the inside leather.

She continued to sit in the chair and stroked the boots as if they were a much loved kitten. For a brief second I saw her hold the open end of a boot to her nose, close her eyes and breathe in. Her lower lips began to tremble ever so slightly and her lovely mouth broadened into a warm smile. She clutched the boots closely to her bosom. I discretely examined the flower vases one more time.

The door to the hall opened and Holmes entered with Reggie-formerly-Theodore. Miss Starlet returned to the central room from the bedroom holding the boots. "He is here. What do we do now?"

"We sit and wait patiently for him to return," said Holmes, "which I expect he will very soon."

"If I may Mr. Holmes, sir," said Reggie. "How did you do it? I know from reading about your accomplishments in *The Strand* that you have used your methods of scientific deduction to lead us here, but please tell me how in the world you came to your conclusions."

"Very well, young man," Holmes replied, "finding your father was quite elementary and I fear will turn out to be the least dangerous portion of this quest we have embarked upon. His banking and legal records showed us that he had lived for a period in London many years ago and there was a reference to a Miss Eugenia Victoria Steward .

"Bonnie. That was the time when he took Bonnie Blue away from Atlanta and lived in London," said Starlet.

"Yes," nodded Holmes, "and he visited or lived in London many times after that. But over two years ago he ceased to conduct his affairs under his own name or initials. He used an assumed name or used someone else to act on his behalf. It would have been futile to look at all of London's hotels asking for Brett Steward since he was not registered under that name.

"From 1893 until 1898 he was a resident at Brown's Hotel, an excellent establishment just around the corner from here in Mayfair. That was obvious from the letterhead he used. Both prior to those dates and afterwards he resided somewhere that supplied him with note paper that bore almost no trace of the name of the hotel, choosing thereby to assure its guests of the utmost in privacy and discretion. However the new owners of this hotel, the Doily Carte family, are too commercially astute not to associate their name with their prestigious guests, so they altered the paper ever so slightly. Here, examine this."

Holmes pulled his glass from one inside pocket and one of the notes that had been sent under the initial "R" and handed them to Reggie. He looked it over closely first with plain eyesight and then using the glass and looked up with a shake of his head and said, "I can't see anything that ties this note to this place."

"Look again," instructed Holmes, "very closely at the very edges of the paper. What do you see?"

"Aha!" cried the young man, "there is the tiniest raised letter 'C' sitting inside a raised circle. The form is like that of the first letter 'C' on the hotel's sign on the street."

"You discern correctly," said Holmes. "The next clue was the name in the register." He turned to Miss Starlet. "You read the list of names. Did not any one of them strike you as being unlike the rest?"

"Not really. Although there was one that struck me as odd." said Miss Starlet, "A 'Baron G. O'Halloran.' Odd only that it was the same last name as my maiden name but it is a very common Irish name and there are thousands of them all over England."

"Ah", said Holmes, "but you will not find a single 'O'Halloran' in Debrett's Peerage. The good Queen, may she rest in peace while instructing God how to better manage the heavens, was not in the habit of bestowing titles of 'Baron' upon the Irish and never upon one of Catholic faith. So permit me to ask you, was your husband fond of your father before his untimely death?"

"He barely knew Pa," replied Miss Starlet, "but he spoke of him with the greatest affection and honour."

"And," Holmes said, "he adopted his name as his own. A mark of respect no doubt. And finally there was the very curious way that the porter gave several sideways glances to you, Reggie. You are reputed to look like your father and there was no doubt that the porter was familiar with your inherited profile but being discrete said nothing that would imperil the renting of rooms at a cost of more than £100 a month for the entire duration of your grand tour. Once you assemble all of these observations, you must then eliminate all of the alternative conclusions. Whatever explanation that you are left with, no matter how improbable, must be the truth. And so here we are. We will wait for Brett Steward and I suspect that he will be along rather soon."

He had no sooner spoken these words than we heard the key turn in the door lock. The person who entered it was not Brett Steward. It was not a man at all. It was a young woman who was holding her matching navy blue bonnet in one hand and examining some letters in the other. She was not as tall as Miss Starlet but still of significant height and bearing and uncommonly attractive. Her hair, released from her bonnet, fell in golden ringlets well below her shoulders. Her complexion was smooth and spoke of excellent health. I guessed that her age would be in her middle twenties.

She looked up and saw us. Her bright blue eyes widened and she made as if to turnaround and run from the room.

"Miss O'Brien," Holmes shouted, "we are here as friends to you and to Brett Steward. My name is Sherlock Holmes and we are gravely concerned for your safety. Please enter and speak with us."

She looked intently at Holmes, appeared to recognize him, and walked directly towards him. She held out her hand and spoke. "I know of your reputation sir and while I have no idea as to how or why you found us I am grateful for your appearance. We are indeed in danger."

"Oh my, are *we* indeed," said Miss Starlet with a tone of sharp sarcasm. "Brett always did prefer his fillies on the young and tender side. Easier to break in and less likely to tire early."

The young woman looked at Miss Starlet. Her face quickly transformed from puzzled to surprised recognition, to a brief flash of a warm smile, and back to one of composed resolution. She strode over to the speaker. "Mrs. Steward, I can assure you that your husband's actions towards me have never been anything but beyond reproach and unquestionably honourable. You may insult me if you wish but in doing so you dishonour your husband and your marriage to him. Brett Steward has only been passionately attracted to one young woman in his entire life and it most certainly is not me, Starlet O'Halloran."

This exchange was followed by a few seconds of intense staring into each other's eyes, which was graciously interrupted by young

Reggie. "Excuse me miss, the other gentleman with Mr. Holmes is his partner, Dr. Watson, and I am Reginald Steward. We apologise for being here unannounced and unsettling you."

The young woman turned towards Reggie and let out a short gasp. She recovered herself and said, "I'm sorry. I did not know that Captain Steward had a son, which looking at you I can only conclude that you must be."

"Yes miss, I am. You could not know about me because my father is not aware of my existence. He never learned of my birth following his departure from Georgia and still knows nothing of my life in spite of the best efforts of my mother to inform him."

The young woman said nothing. She continued to look at Reggie. Her face evidenced a feeling of sorrow and I thought I saw a tear forming in her eye. She walked slowly over to one of the chairs, sat down and buried her head in her hands and slowly shook it back and forth causing her lovely long golden tresses to sway.

A few moments later she raised her head and with a tone of confidence spoke to us. "Forgive me. The past few days have been very trying and I have been quite terrified. Three men with whom I have done business over the past several years have all been murdered and I am in fear of my life, and Captain Steward's. For reasons I cannot tell you I have not asked the police for their help and your presence is a godsend."

I had no doubt that the words she spoke to us were true, but there was also no doubt that her emotional collapse a few moments ago was occasioned by her being informed about the hitherto unknown son of Brett Steward and not just her concern for safety.

"Perhaps you could tell us then how it is that you are connected to Captain Steward," said Holmes, "but before doing so allow me to wish you a happy birthday which I gather is either today or tomorrow." The young woman stared in amazement at Sherlock Holmes with the same look as I have seen on the faces of countless women when they discovered that he knew far more about them than was humanly possible for any normal man to know.

"It would seem that the famous detective already knows more than I could have expected, so I will give you the briefest summary before Captain Steward returns.

"My father, Connor O'Brien and Brett Steward were fellow soldiers of fortune. They met in the Sudan and became great friends and comrades-in-arms. Both were men of unflinching principles who believed in fighting as they said..."

"For lost causes once they're really lost," interrupted Miss Starlet. "I remember hearing that line the night I watched the Old South disappear. Please continue miss."

"They consulted with kings and peasants, with bishops and prisoners of conscience, with all types so long as they believed them to be honourable and acting in the selfless pursuit of liberty and freedom. They provided them with the arms and ammunition they needed to fight their oppressors. Some of those they helped were victorious. Most were not. Many times they came close to death themselves but always managed to use their wits and courage to escape, except for one time in India when, according to your husband, Mrs. Steward, he was under fire and expected to die when my father came to his rescue.

"Sadly my father was grievously wounded. Captain Steward was able to get the two of them to safety and on board a ship back to England. My father did not survive and was buried at sea. Captain Steward informed me that my father's last words to him were to tell him that he had a young daughter whose mother had died in childbirth while living under the Raj. My father beseeched his dearest friend to look after his Briany, for that is my name, and after his death I became an orphan. Captain Steward made certain I was well looked after by the St. Andrew's Mission that was caring for orphans in Calcutta. Under the guidance of the sainted Rev. Dr. John Graham, the mission soon established a wonderful home for children in the village of Kalimpong, in the beauty of the Hill Country.

"Captain Steward never failed to visit me once a term and always sent gifts at Christmas and for my birthday. Several times he took me on the little Darjeelng Railway down to Siliguri and back.

"I wanted to make him proud of me and so I worked very diligently at all my studies and at my sports. When I turned eighteen I graduated from the school, which we all affectionately called Dr. Graham's Homes, and came to live in England. He arranged for me to be tutored by his friends Beatrice and Sidney Webb at their newly founded school, the London School of Economics.

"Upon completion of my studies Captain Steward appointed me as his business manager and I carried out transactions in his name. Two years ago events of which I cannot speak took place that forced him to become very secretive about his actions and whereabouts and so I assumed responsibility for his affairs. That is my position today. My rooms are across the hall, however I work from here during business hours. And so here I am gentlemen, and madam."

With this she stopped. Holmes had listened intently in his familiar pose of pressing his fingertips together. After a moment's silence he spoke to her in a kindly manner. "Miss Briany, you are assured that we will do everything we can to protect you but if we are to be able to help, you must be willing to be forthright about your close relationship with Captain Steward. It is well beyond that of his being your patron and now employer . You have left out an important point."

Briany looked at Sherlock Holmes, then at Miss Starlet and finally at Reggie. When she spoke the volume was subdued and filled with quiet emotion, "My father asked his friend not only to look after his motherless daughter. He also implored him not to let me grow up as an orphan. Captain Steward took the necessary legal steps and adopted me as his daughter. Since I was ten years of age Brett Steward has been my father." With this she stopped her narrative and took several deep breaths. "He has been the most loving and at the same time demanding father that I could ever ask God to give me.

"He spoke of you often, Miss Starlet, and has continued to be passionately in love with you but knew the two of you could never live together without, as he said, a re-enactment of the War Between the States. He had decided some time ago to return to Atlanta when he turned sixty-five years of age but the events to which I referred earlier took over and made that impossible. Once these current troubles are resolved I believe he would wish to come home.

"He refused to open and read your letters knowing that if he did he would be overcome with his feelings for you and come running back to Clayton County only to make life miserable for both of you. So he instructed me to write "Whereabouts Unknown" on them and mail them back to you. It was for this reason, my returning of your letters, that he never learned that he had a son." With this she turned to Reggie and said, "I am so very sorry for depriving you of your father, and he of his son, and I pray for yours and God's forgiveness. It was not my intent." She returned her gaze to Miss Starlet.

"I am aware Mrs. Steward that you and your husband had a daughter, Eugenia Victoria. You called her Bonnie Blue and she died so tragically. I did not in any way replace her in your husband's affections. If anything my presence in his life was a constant and deeply painful reminder of your loss. He often said that I caused him to think about what your daughter might have been like had she not been taken from you. Our ages and physical attributes were, he said, quite similar. Although in the past few years he had often said that I have become so headstrong that I now remind him of you, Mrs.

Steward. I have considered that the most admiring and loving compliment he could ever give me.

"I trust with all my heart that you will be able to bear the news I have imparted and to make the best of things for the future, for it would appear that under the law you are now my mother, and I am your daughter. And you, young sir," she said turning to Reggie, "are my brother and I cannot begin to express the joy I am feeling in my heart having met you, and you, Miss Starlet, although I cannot hide from the pain I have caused you."

For a minute no one spoke as they took in this information..

"Well now," said Miss Starlet, "did not some writer say that unhappy families were all unhappy in their own way? I must say that ours will be truly one of a kind. So enough of the tears, my dear. Do not place any blame on yourself. Fiddle-dee-dee. Children are never the cause of family misfortune. It was Brett and I who brought all of this on ourselves and on you." Here she paused.

"As God is my witness, we shall do a better job from here on."

She paused again, lost it seemed in memory and reflection. "I do believe that the last time I spoke those words I was holding a carrot in my one hand and my other fist up to the sky. It was not my finest hour. But if I think about those days too long I will go mad. So let us get on with things. Should not father be coming home for lunch by now?"

She said these words and suddenly her eyes widened, as did those of Reggie and Briany. Holmes and I had our backs to the balcony doors and as I turned to see what they were looking at I found myself looking down the barrel of a revolver. A similar gun was held to the head of Sherlock Holmes. The holder of the guns was a tall man, impeccably dressed, broad shouldered and with silver hair. He had silently entered over the balcony and there was no escaping from his revolver. "Do not move a muscle or I will blow both of your brains out," he firmly told us.

CHAPTER FOUR - BRETT

"Really Brett, darling," spoke Miss Starlet from across the room, "you must try to be more welcoming and gracious to our guests. We have so few of them come to call these days. Please, my dear husband, allow me to introduce your newest business associates, Dr. John Watson and Mr. Sherlock Holmes. I have engaged their services for the protection of our family and I have invited them to stay for lunch. We were all just waiting for you."

The look on our assailant's face was beyond description.

There was the shock of disbelief, followed by a warm and loving broad smile and a slow shaking of his head. The words came slowly from him.

"Starlet . . . O'Halloran," he said slowly and deliberately, "Starlet . . . O'Halloran, this is indeed a surprise and you are even more ravishingly beautiful then I remember." His laid down his revolvers walked slowly across the room, reached out for his wife's hand, dropped to one knee and lightly touched his lips to her fingers.

Brett rose to his feet and looked spellbound upon Miss Starlet. There was an awkwardness to them, such as a young man and woman might experience on their first outing without a chaperon, neither of them prepared to make the first move towards touching each other's bodies.

This embarrassed silence continued until Briany spoke up. "For goodness sakes, Father. She's your wife. She didn't cross the Atlantic to be stared at. Embrace her!" Both Brett and Miss Starlet smiled and threw their arms around each other. They stood there for some time with their eyes closed, lost in the intense feelings they still shared for each other.

Without letting go of Miss Starlet, Brett opened his eyes and raised his head. He smiled warmly at his daughter and then glanced at the other young person in the room. His eyes widened when they landed on Reggie and he dropped his embrace of his wife. The young man walked up to his father, stopped a few feet away, snapped the heels of his boots together, stood at attention, and gave a salute. "Good morning, father. Reginald Gerald Steward reporting for duty sir. I believe we are serving in the same regiment."

Brett was again stunned into silence. He looked at Reggie, seeing what was undeniably a version of himself fifty years ago. He looked at Miss Starlet who smiled at him with forced sweetness, pointed a finger first at Reggie and then at Brett, and said "He's . . .yours."

For what seemed an eternity no one spoke. Brett stood dumbly looking back and forth from Miss Starlet to Reggie. He turned and walked vacantly towards the balcony. As he approached the edge he held out both his hands and placed them on the railing, lowering his head until we could only see his broad back. After several minutes he raised his head and looked up into the cloudy sky. He turned and walked back into the room.

With a courtesy that was unfeigned he said, "In my three-score and ten years on this earth I have consistently followed my heart and my passion for causes that I believed to be righteous. Behind that bravado I confess that I believed in Brett Steward, the only cause I really knew. What was it you used to call me Starlet – 'a conceited, black-hearted varmint, a low-down, cowardly, nasty thing.' Perhaps you were right. But against all odds the good Lord has blessed me with a beautiful wife and now a son. I have badly neglected my duties as a father. I assure you that that will not happen again and I will do my best, the good Lord willin', to make up for years that have been lost and cannot be lived over again. I do hope that you will join me, son, in doing so."

Reggie looked his father in the eye and replied, "Yes sir, it will be an honour, but only if you acknowledge that you have also neglected your duties as a husband and assure your wife that you will strive to make up for those years as well."

Brett looked at the young man who had just so firmly rebuked his father. He lifted his head as if to speak to the heavens, "Good Lord. I cannot escape divine retribution. My son has my ears and his mother's tongue. My seventy year-old heart may not be up to this."

"Your seventy-year old heart is just fine, father." This time is was his daughter that spoke. "You can still ride and run with men half your age. I've seen you. It's well past time you stopped chasing lost causes and that we all just got on with the business of being a family."

He looked steadfastly at Briany and sighed, "*Et tu, Brutè?* You are entirely correct, my dear.'

He gazed slowly at the three members of his family. "Once again I find that I have to ask for your forgiveness in the hope that we could give our life together another chance. And I seek no greater grace for my old age than being surrounded by those I love and will learn to love."

The warm smile faded from his face. "Unfortunately for all of us those days will still have to be postponed but perhaps only for a week. Events are quickly conspiring not only against us, but against all that is good and decent in western civilization. Gentlemen," he said turning to Holmes and me, "I thank you for your offer of protection and your diligent work in finding me. I had thought I had covered my tracks more successfully. Concerning my present situation I can only say that Fortune, it now appears, is no longer on the side of the strongest battalion but on the side of the most utterly ruthless. I am afraid that I am involved in dangerous affairs to which you all cannot be privy."

"I assume," said Sherlock Holmes, "that you are referring to the nefarious plans of the Black Hand to assassinate the crown prince in conjunction with the coronation ceremony this Saturday?"

Brett stared severely at Holmes "Yes," he said, "that is precisely what I am referring to. And please tell me sir how it is that you came to know of this. The only other three men who knew about it are now all dead, their personal connection to me having somehow become known."

"In normal times," explained Holmes, "a gentleman would never read another gentleman's mail. But these are not normal times and I read through the file your now deceased solicitor kept for you, as well as the contents of his unreliable safe, and I managed to cross-question his staff and had them tell me all they knew about his and your undertakings. They did so knowing that they could not possibly do him any harm and with the hope and prayer that it might help to bring his murderers to justice."

"Well then," said Brett, "it would appear that we find ourselves fighting for the same cause." Brett graciously motioned for the group of us to be seated.

Sherlock Holmes spoke first. "While I have been able to synthesize much of the data, there are many facets of your story that I do not yet know, so pray you, sir, please enlighten us as to how it is we find you here and engaged in this most dangerous pursuit."

Brett began to speak in the manner that Americans refer to as the Charleston cadence, that slow and pleasant drawl that is so often associated with a gentleman of The South.

"For fifty years I have been a soldier of fortune, fighting for 'the Cause' and for people I believed to be truly good. My doing so has had costs beyond what I ever could have imagined. Even now I am looking at my so recently restored family knowing that I have endangered the lives of another five people."

"Six Brett darling," Miss Starlet interjected, "we cannot forget that Momma is with us."

Brett's face broke into a wide grin. "Momma? You mean to tell me that she is alive and well and here with you in London?"

"Yes, my dear. She is waiting for us at the hotel. She would not hear of my travelling abroad in search of you without her. She is quite ready to grab you firmly by the ear and march you back to The South where you belong," Miss Starlet said.

"Well now, I'll be . . . I do expect that will happen very soon. Very soon indeed. And she still won't like me. But let me finish a short version of my long story.

"As I helped to find fighters and get them organized in some sort of army I from time to time would meet small groups of men and one or two women who had joined our ranks but who seemed woefully ignorant of who or why we were fighting or what we were dreaming of. They were fixin' only to bring wrack and ruin to whatever dynasty was in power, no matter what the cost in lives lost and property.

"They weren't revolutionaries. They were just anarchists. They had all read their Marx, and Kropotkin and Bakunin and they just wanted to smash the system. Some of them were all talk, but others were good mercenaries and brave fighters. And there were a few of them who were utterly ruthless; no conscience at all. They would sneak up behind enemy lines at night and murder and mutilate old men and women, mothers and children. They did so without a scrap of remorse, claiming that "sparing the nit breeds the louse." Whenever the opportunity arose they would souce out the leaders of the other side - their politicians, their priests, and their generals - and assassinate them in the cruelest ways they could think of.

"Over the years I began to see these men reappear in the ranks of the fighters that I had recruited. One year they would be in Hungary, the next year in Venezuela, the year after that in India. Most said little or nothing to me and didn't do much talkin' at all. But I befriended a few of them and over time they spilled the beans and told me their secrets.

"I got to know about the inner workings of an organization they called Black Hand." Here he paused and looked at Holmes.

"You appear to have become familiar with them, Mr. Holmes. In Holland and the Cape they are *zwarte hand*, in Spain *mano neare,* in the Balkans they call themselves *oopa pika,* and in France *main noire.* They all know each other and over time I came to know many of their names and the forty or more cells of them that are scattered around the world. I made some records and eventually I put together a list of most of their active members."

"Surely, " I asked, "you took that list to the Home Office or Whitehall and had them round these men up, did you not?"

"Ah, Doctor Watson, I regret to inform you that such a move does not come easily when you are *persona non gratia* to many of Her Majesty's civil servants. You see I made a point of fighting for whichever side I believed in, not just the one with the friendliest flag. More than once that left me fighting *against* your Empire, not defending it. I went to the Cape thinking of helping the British Army overcome the guerilla tactics of the Boers. What I found was that Kitchener was violating all types of international law and basic human decency by rounding up the Boers' women and children, forcing them into concentration camps, and starving them to death. So I changed sides and began to run the British naval blockades and provide arms to the Boers. You can guess that this did not endear me to either your politicians or your generals. So I find myself in the rather unenviable position of now seeking to protect an Empire against the forces of anarchy even though that Empire dislikes me and I it."

"If ," asked Holmes, "you bear no affection for the British Empire why sir are you risking your life to protect it?"

"Your Empire, Mr. Holmes, ain't worth a pitcher of warm piss," said Brett forcefully, "but the stability it brings to the world is a necessary evil. If it were to crumble and start fighting with the decaying French, Austro-Hungarian, Russian or Ottoman Empires all of Europe and the colonies around the world would become one massive bloodbath, the likes of which history has never known, bigger than even the tragic losses of our war for the Independence of the Confederate States.

"All it would take would be the assassination of some king or queen of one country that could be blamed on another and your whole house of cards would come tumbling down. The Black Hand tried to kill the Prince a couple of years back in Belgium. Before that they made attempts on the Czar. Thank heaven these failed.

"Now they have plans to kill the Prince of Wales either just before or after he is crowned this Saturday and make it look as if were ordered by that silly young fool, Wilhelm, in Germany. If they succeed it will unleash tragedy beyond belief. Scotland Yard and

Whitehall will not listen to me. The only chance I have is to stop these evil bastards myself."

"I do understand, however," said Holmes, "that you have at least one significant person who has listened to you, whose coat of arms appeared often in your private correspondence."

"Quite right, Mr. Holmes. My dear old friend, Bertie, better known as the Prince of Wales and soon to be King, has been my confident and drinking partner since I hauled him out of a whorehouse, sobered him up and got him back to Sandringham a couple of decades ago. But he is proud and pig-headed and refuses to cancel his ride to the coronation in an open carriage where his subjects can cheer on their sovereign. He believes that he will be safe merely because he will be surrounded by thousands of ordinary blokes who would never let any harm come to him. He knows about the Black Hand but has no appreciation for their cunning and cold-blooded ruthlessness."

"Perhaps we can offer some reassurance," said Holmes. "While you may be on the outs with our constabulary I am not entirely. Even if I am far from their favourite consulting detective they have come to respect my work. If I were to suggest to them that not only might someone attempt to assassinate the King right under their noses, but that their prized reputations would be trampled in the dust if even a failed attempt were to occur, they would start scampering about like mice very quickly. If might also be useful for you to know that my wonderful regiment of spies have discovered the places where the five members of your cell of anarchists are staying. We may be able to round them up before they get to the spectacle on Saturday."

Brett looked intently at Holmes and gave a slow nod of appreciation. "Both of those actions would be very helpful, sir. If I could be assured that you could bring those to pass then I might even be able to relax for an hour or two and enjoy some time with my family."

"A well-deserved opportunity, I agree," said Holmes. "But I must caution you all to assume some sort of disguise before re-entering the Dorchester. Your enemies will have a lookout watching for you.

"Thank you, Sherlock," said Miss Starlet. "I have no doubt you will take whatever steps are needed for our safety and the preservation of your Empire. We will just hide ourselves at the Dorchester and, Lord willing, my family will book passage next week to return to a life together in America. Perhaps I am assuming too much," she added looking at Briany. "I do hope that my recently acquired daughter will be coming with us."

The young woman smiled at her. "I grew up in the warm lush climate of Calcutta and the Hill Country. I would welcome the opportunity to live with my mother, father, and brother in the lovely warmth of Georgia. I have not seen the sun in the past two weeks. Have you?"

They chuckled, and Brett added, "Sweetheart, don't speak too soon, you have yet to meet Momma."

With that Miss Starlet and Reggie laughed and the four of them all looked warmly at each other.

"Come Watson," said Holmes rising. "We have some business to do with Lestrade and we are not needed at this family reunion."

With that we rose and said our good-byes. Before he could exit the room Miss Starlet threw her arms around Holmes's body, held him tightly for several moments and planted a kiss on his cheek, leaving a telltale mark of lipstick. I have never seen Holmes looking so utterly discomfited and could not wait to recount the incident to Mrs. Hudson.

CHAPTER FIVE - KING'S LYNN

We hailed a cab outside Claridges and Holmes gave the driver instructions for the route he wished to take to the Embankment and the offices of Scotland Yard. We backtracked several blocks so that we could ride down the length of The Mall from Buckingham Palace to Westminster Abbey, the route of the coronation procession on Saturday, and where any would-be assassin could be lurking amidst the throngs of Londoners, who, being English, would be sure to turn out regardless of whatever miserable weather would be visited upon them.

Holmes made notes as we went, jotting down the locations in which a sniper could hide himself or those spots along the route where the curb was precariously close to the narrow roadway and where an attacker could come within a few feet of the passing open carriage. He seemed satisfied with his observations.

"Inspector Lestrade and his men may be lacking in imagination, Watson, but they are quite experienced in the management of crowds. He undoubtedly could have men in plain clothes scattered throughout. Even if we are not able to round up the evil bastards, as our Mr. Steward calls them, there will be adequate protection from the Palace to the Abbey. Following the service the King will be in a closed carriage and taken quickly to Windsor, so there is not much worry there."

The cab pulled into the new headquarters of Scotland Yard. Holmes and I entered and sought out our earnest if not always brilliant colleague, Inspector Lestrade.

He did not so much as agree to our meeting with him as looked annoyed at us as we barged into his office, sat ourselves down, and began the meeting without seeking his consent. As he was wont to do, his first reaction was to dismiss Holmes's warning as yet another of his far-fetched imaginings.

"Really Mr. Holmes," he protested, "you cannot expect me to lay on hundreds more constables, who were themselves looking forward to taking their children to view the parade, just because Mr. Sherlock Holmes has come up with yet another plot wherein an evil web of a few hundred people with revolvers are about to topple five empires and usher in Armageddon."

Holmes retained his patience, developed by many such similar encounters with Lestrade, and with firm evidence and undeniable logic laid out his case. As he did I watched the smirk retreat from Lestrade's face and be replaced with a look of wide-eyed fear. His knuckles gripped the arms of his chair tightly. By the time Holmes was finished Lestrade was on his feet and shouting orders out of his door for his lackeys and his lackeys' lackeys to hustle into his office.

"As you say that all of these men are armed and skilled in the use of weapons, Holmes, I will organize a raid upon the places you say they are boarding in the hours just before dawn. That is when we are most likely to find criminals sound asleep and the fewest bystanders in danger should we have to engage in an exchange of gunfire. However, I expect that by six o'clock in the morning we shall have them all rounded up and securely locked up in the Old Bailey waiting to appear before a judge."

Holmes nodded his consent and we departed. "I really see nothing else we can do, my dear Watson. Our client and her family will have to make accommodations with their multiple ferocious personalities if they are to get along. We brought them together and that was our task. Scotland Yard and the bobbies should be able to manage to protect the King. As is normal with these cases no one shall hear about our efforts and Lestrade will take all the credit for imprisoning the garrotters, but we shall know what we have done. And so I suggest that we visit Marcini's in Knightsbridge and reward ourselves with a little dinner. What say you, Watson?"

I heartily agreed. We enjoyed a long mealtime, and took in a concert at the Royal Albert Hall, where a lovely contralto, one of Holmes many former acquaintances, delivered an excellent Tosca, thrilling the audience before hurling herself from the parapet. Even Holmes was moved to his feet in sustained applause.

We retired to Baker Street and fell into bed with that feeling of tired satisfaction that comes from knowing that you have done your job well.

And all was well.

At least it was until five o'clock in the morning when there was an unholy pounding on the door of 221B Baker Street. "Mr. Holmes! Mr. Holmes!" we heard a boy's voice shouting. "Mr. Holmes! You must come!" The pounding was loud and desperate. I wrapped myself in my dressing gown and entered our parlour. Holmes appeared in his gown close behind me. We began down the stairs only to see that the redoubtable Mrs. Hudson was already at the door and holding the young captain of the Irregulars by the back of his jacket to restrain him from bounding up the stairs.

"Let the lad up," said Holmes, whereupon he was released and leapt up the stairs taking two or three at a time. We met him in the parlour.

He was gasping to catch his breath. He had no doubt run some distance at a very fast pace and was soaked to the skin from the never-ending rain.

"Those men, those men you told us to watch Mr. Holmes. Those four blokes and the small boy. You told us never to let them out our sight, right, well we done that. But a hour ago they all got up an out their places. They was in four different inns, they were, an they walked through the night an all met up at Paddington an they gots themselves tickets an they left. My boys followed them all the way an then they run back to me an wake me up, an then I come running to you, Mr. Holmes."

Holmes looked at the boy with a look of grave concern, "Did your boys learn what train they were taking. What was the destination? Did anyone hear what tickets they asked for?"

"One o' my boys, sir, Jimmy, the wee one that's not afraid of no one, he follows them right to the ticket office pretendin' to be a beggar, an he hears them askin' for tickets to Nor'ich. All five of them. The four men and the boy with 'em. They got on the early train to Nor'ich. Jimmy an the rest they waits until they see them board an then they come runnin' for me and then I come runnin' for you, Mr. Holmes, sir."

"You and your boys have done well Gordon," said Holmes, clasping his hand on the lad's shoulder. "Better than you may ever know. Now I have another urgent task for you and you must not fail. You are to run from here to the Dorchester Hotel. You know it do you not? On Park Lane."

"Sure an I know it sir. But they would never let me anywhere close to comin' in. The maids would be chasin' me with brooms all the way to Hyde Park Corner if I was to ever set foot in it."

"Gordon, I do not care a fig how many maids there are with brooms, or what you have to do to get past them, and it would be best if you never tell me how you did it, but you must get a message to the guests in suite 615. Can you do that Gordon?"

A grin that in other circumstances I would only describe as mischievous bordering on wicked spread over the lad's face. He nodded. "I can do that for sure, sir. Long as you don't never ask how I done it."

"Excellent. Tell the guests in that suite exactly what you have told me, and demand that both Mr. Steward senior and his son be ready to be picked up at the front door in an hour. Tell them to make a quick run over to Mr. Steward senior's residence and get his weapons. Do you have all that? Good. Now run like you had three bobbies on your tail."

Descending seventeen stairs in three steps is a skill that only the young can risk. Gordon was off and out the door and on his way. I smiled at him but Holmes was fearfully distraught.

"Dear God, Watson. How could I have not foreseen this. These villains are much too clever to try to shoot the King with thousands of onlookers and police throughout the crowd." He paused. "Either that or Lestrade has a spy in his troops. No matter. I should have known that this would happen."

"What is going to happen, Holmes? What!?" I came near to shouting back to him.

"Can't you see Watson? They are not going to assassinate the King on the final leg of the coronation procession. They are going for the first leg. In Norfolk. As he leaves Sandringham. We have to get ourselves there to stop them. How could I not have seen this coming?"

Sandringham, on the grand estate in Norfolk, was one of the homes of the Royal Family. The Prince of Wales, soon to be the King, had lived there for the past four decades, from the time of his marriage to Alexandra when he was twenty-one until the present. He had held legendary parties, hunting outings, banquets and drinking bouts that lasted days and were rumoured to have been attended by countless women whose morals were a matter of convenience. The Crown Prince, once called by his Christian names of Albert Edward and known by all as Bertie, was spending his last few days there before his coronation and his move to Buckingham Palace. He did not care for Buck Place for the simple reason that his mother did not care for him, and never forgave him for bringing about the untimely early death of his father the Prince Consort. The Prince was said to have risen unwisely from his sick bed and hurried himself off to some seaside resort where young Bertie was cavorting openly with a married woman and threatening to bring shame upon the entire House of Hanover. The Consort took very seriously ill after the stressful journey and passed away soon after. The Queen blamed Bertie for the next thirty years.

"Watson, we must move quickly," said Holmes as he studied the railway schedule. "There is not another train from London to Norwich until ten o'clock. That will be too late."

"Too late for what Holmes. What are they going to do?"

"Here. Look here!" he said handing me *The Times*. 'Read what is going there *today! Within a few hours!*"

On the front page was a short piece that read:

Affectionate Sendoff from Norfolk to be the First Stop of the Coronation Celebration

Citizens of King's Lynn in Norfolk all know that the coronation procession of King Edward VII will not begin at Buckingham Palace but rather at the train station in their village. For it is from there that the new King will begin the journey that will end with a crown being placed on his head in Westminster Abbey. For forty years the Prince of Wales was a much-loved favourite of this corner of the land. While his great gatherings and parties may have raised eyebrows at the Court of St. James, the townspeople knew that they brought well-heeled folks from around the world who needed food and lodging, carriage and horse rentals, demands for all sorts of trades and medical attention. The Prince, Bertie to all and sundry, will be missed sorely.

They will not let him depart however without a "Royal Sendoff" and have organized their own short coronation parade through the village in an open carriage, drawn by six of the Prince's glorious horses. Not only the merchants but also the many railway workers who serviced his private car for so many years, and the dock hands who made sure that his yacht was securely fastened and kept gleaming at its berth on the canal, will be there to give rousing best wishes to their loved and generous patron.

The carriage parade is scheduled to begin at noon at the north end of the village and end at the station twenty – five minutes after. The Prince and soon to be King will then have a few moments in his private car before it pulls out on its journey to London at precisely 12:45 pm.

"That is where they are going to strike." said Holmes. "The chubby old chap will be a sitting duck for any assassin. The roads are narrow and there cannot be more than a few hundred people to line the route. The train will not get us there before the Black Hand. We shall have to find the fastest coach-and-four available and get there in time to stop them."

"Cannot we just send a telegram to the local police?" I asked.

"There is only one constable in a village that size. Reinforcements from London will need as much time as we will going by train. Mrs. Hudson! Mrs. Hudson!" Holmes had opened the door and shouted for our long-suffering landlady. She appeared in a moment still in her dressing gown but wide awake as a result of the incident restraining the nimble Gordon.

"My dear Mrs. Hudson," began Holmes.

"Enough of the pleasantries Mr. Holmes, I can see by the look on your face that something desperate is taking place. What do you need this time?"

"A coach-and-four. The fastest you can find. Immediately. And thank you."

"Very well," she said. She pulled her mackintosh on over her nightgown and off she went into the rain and early morning gloom. I was somewhat concerned that she would catch cold on so foul a morning but I had also learned that there were few things that so warmed her blood as being able to play an essential if small role in the adventures of her famous tenant.

Holmes pulled an atlas off the shelf and began to study the maps of Norfolk.

"Our villains are taking the train to Norwich and then will have to change and take the Great Eastern over to King's Lynn.," he said,

"We can ride hard, change horses at Newmarket, and then go due north bypassing Norwich. That should give us a chance to gain at least an hour on them, maybe two. We shall have to try to pick up their trail from the King's Lynn station, which is the station that serves Sandringham. The locals should be willing to give us whatever information we need. Do you have your service revolver, Watson?"

"It is already in my pocket and I have an ammunition pouch on my belt."

"Excellent. I shall do the same and let us hope that our dear Mrs. Hudson is as efficient as she usually is."

Ten minutes later we heard the loud clatter of a large coach and the sounds of a team of horses, and then a shrill whistle. "They hardly have to whistle for us," objected an annoyed Holmes. "We are not deaf nor street urchins. Surely Mrs. Hudson could have stopped that unnecessary nonsense."

We descended the stairs. Mrs. Hudson held the door open for us and as I passed her she opened her fist just enough for me to see a small whistle. She gave me a small wink and I daresay I felt her hand giving a firm pat to my backside as I moved through the door.

"Come Watson, the game has become much more dangerous and our adversaries are far more devious than I gave them credit for. Haste, driver! To the Dorchester and do not spare the horses."

It was only a few blocks from Baker Street to Park Lane and with the streets still deserted in the early morning hours we were there in a few minutes. Brett Steward and his son, standing proudly beside his father, were waiting at the front door, with a wooden case of a foot square and five feet long on the pavement beside them. Together they hoisted it up to the top of the coach and with the help of the driver tied it down. Father and son may have not been present in each other's lives for the past seventeen years but there was a bond of blood between them and they moved like a well-trained team. They had already become comrades-in-arms and seemed beyond eager to enter battle shoulder-to-shoulder.

I felt exhilarated; the prospect of adventure and thrill of battle coursing through my veins, as only a man can when he marches with his trusted fellow soldiers into the cannon's roar.

My lovely feeling vanished in an instant when to my shock and dismay Miss Starlet and Miss O'Brien emerged from the hotel lobby and climbed into the coach with me. I gasped and shouted to Brett, "You cannot possibly be allowing these women to come on this journey. We are up against highly trained and ruthless foes. This will be no place for a woman!"

Brett looked at me and gave me a warm smile displaying his gleaming white teeth. "Yes sir. They are coming along. Best soldiers I ever trained. I've always admired their spirits, especially when they're cornered. I wouldn't want to be in their sights at two hundred yards and I for sure would not want to be in the hand-to-hand combat zone with them and neither would you if you value your life or your manhood."

I looked at Sherlock Holmes, desperate for some moral support. He just shrugged and said, "If the Captain says so, then we can use the additional force. Let us be off."

Mrs. Hudson had found us an excellent coach. There was adequate room in the carriage and it was well sprung. We moved as quickly as we could through the streets of London until we reached the Victoria Embankment. The road was clear along the Thames and so we galloped all the way to Whitechapel, turned north, and after working our way through the streets of the east end we entered the open countryside and the driver gave the horses free rein.

The farms and the scattered houses flashed past us as we looked out the windows. We were constantly being jostled and from time to time would hit a bump in the road and we would all take a jump into the air before landing back on our seats. Miss Starlet was seated beside her husband with her arm through his and from time to time I could hear snatches of a little ditty she was singing to herself:

She wept with delight at his smile
And trembled with fear at his frown

She seemed serenely happy.

On the opposite bench Briany and Reggie were chattering away like long lost brother and sister, all on fire to catch up on the years they had missed.

Holmes kept jotting notes and starring at maps. I had seen him this way before many times. His inscrutable mind was making sure that there was not one detail that would be missed. He had already been fooled once by this diabolical crew. He was resolute that it would not happen again.

By eight o'clock we were at Newmarket and we stopped and changed horses. To my joy the rain had finally stopped and the sun was shining. Holmes had no appreciation of Nature at all but the rest of us breathed in the beauty. The mists were rising off the fields and the warmth of the sun on my face led me to think that perhaps the climate of our green and pleasant land was not entirely intolerable. And what a perfect day for the good people of King's Lynn to bid farewell to their favourite member of the Royal Family, or it would be if we could keep the man from being shot.

From Newmarket we took the secondary road towards the north. The road was not as good and the ride much more rugged but still we flew along. The conversations had died down. We knew we were approaching some highly treacherous waters. Within the next few hours either we would be dead along with the King, or some determined evil doers would be thwarted and either killed or in jail. There was no more laughter.

The coach pulled into the railway station at King's Lynn at just past ten o'clock. We had a mere two hours to find the killers and stop them.

Holmes immediately went to the station office and we stood on the platform waiting for him. A few minutes later he returned to us. "Watson, I do apologise for the times I have accused you of exaggerating my exploits in your stories. Because of you, my dear friend, even the station master in King's Lynn has been reading them and was prepared to help in any way he could if it meant being part of a murderous mystery. He knows the men we are looking for. They have been staying in the village off and on for the past three months but not near the central square. They have rented a cottage some three miles out that looks over the canal. There is no road to it, only a trail. So we cannot take the coach. There is a livery man in the village who is said to be a churlish piece of work but has excellent horses that he has rented for years to guests of the Prince, and is quite happy to rent to anyone now that the Prince's sycophants have departed. We will have to unload our gun case and carry the weapons we need with us."

Brett and Reggie moved immediately and lifted down the heavy case. It had a strong metal hinged handle on both ends and they each clasped one, lifted the case and began walking into the village. Upon arrival at the livery stable Holmes approached a rather surly looking chap and enquired about horses to rent. His price was high but the animals were very impressive and obviously well-cared for.

"It'll take me an hour to saddle up six of them. You can come back when I'm ready," he said.

I was ready to speak reasonably to the man but before I could young Reggie walked up to him and with a smile laid a hand on the much smaller man's shoulder and said, "Well now, sir, we just don't happen to have an hour so I tell you what's going to happen. You're just going to stand aside and we're going to get those saddles on those horses ourselves. I'm sure that's going to be real okay with you."

The gnarly little fellow looked up at the large young man but had no time to speak before Reggie was striding towards the tack room and saying to the rest of us, "We can all grab us a bridle, blanket and saddle, it's all here. Let's get going." Brett stood beaming at him and Miss Starlet stole a moment of sliding her arm through Brett's and looking proudly at her son.

Each of us marched into the tack room, took what we needed, chose ourselves a horse and saddled up. I was surprised to see the two ladies firmly clasp the back of their horse's mouth, force it open and slide the bit into place. In England a lady will normally wait for a groom to do that job for her, but then these were not normal ladies. They both chose men's saddle, not ladies', placed their blankets on the horse's backs and swung the saddles up and into place. As Miss Starlet reached under her horse to grab the cinch belt her spirited beast gave her a firm bump with its haunches causing her to land on her backside on the floor of the stable.

"Hey there, mother, you got yourself one who thinks she's in charge," said Reggie with a laugh. Miss Starlet got up and said, "We'll see about that." She took a step back and gave a swift firm kick to the mare's midsection. The horse gave a whinny of pain. She then walked to the front of the horse, pulled on its bridle and looked the beast directly in the eye. "Do you want that again? Do you? Didn't think so." With that she cinched up the strap and pulled it tight.

Reggie, Brett, and Sherlock were already up on their mounts. "Sweetheart," Brett said to Briany, "would you mind handing us up the guns and rifles?" Briany opened the gun case and gave each of them a set of holstered pistols and a gleaming new Mauser 98 rifle. They fastened the holsters around their waists and slung the rifles over their shoulders. I had to remark that they looked like men who were not to be trifled with.

"We three shall go first to the small tavern that is closest to the rented cottage," said Holmes. "I will try to find out from the publican if our adversaries are in the cottage. We shall meet you there." With this they rode off. It was now already 10:30 am.

Briany, Miss Starlet, and I were about to lead our mounts out of the stable and into the courtyard when the surly livery man slouched towards the doorway, blocking our exit. "I must have made a mistake in the price I said you would have to pay. I will need one more sovereign from each of you or I will not permit you leave my property with my horses."

"Why you miserable cheat and coward," I shouted at him. "We paid you a fair price and you have so little courage that you waited until those three men had departed before trying to swindle us. You will not have one penny more. Now move your miserable self and let us be on our way."

"You may call me what you wish, but you will not leave my premises with my horses until you pay me. I assure you that the law is on my side," he snarled back at me.

"Please Doctor Watson," Miss Starlet spoke in what I detected as feigned sweetness. "What is one more sovereign to us? Besides we are in a hurry. Sir, come, take your money and let us be on our way."

"Glad you sees things my way," the miserable cheat said as he walked toward Miss Starlet. She reached inside her jacket and withdrew her purse, and opened it. By this time the surly knave was just a few feet away from her. With a very fast move Miss Starlet swung her leg forward and planted a hard kick in the man's groin. His mouth opened and he let forth a roar of pain. His two hands immediately grasped his nether region and he collapsed on the stable floor, writhing in pain. Instead of withdrawing sovereigns from her purse Miss Starlet produced a small stiletto dagger and placed the end of it a short distance inside the blackguard's left nostril. The terror in his eyes was pitiable.

"We paid you a fair price and I have no patience with cheats and liars," said Miss Starlet. "We will return within a few hours with your horses and we thank you for your service."

As I walked past the wretch I swear I heard him mutter something about "God dammed Americans. I should have known."

CHAPTER SIX - THE BLACK HAND

The two women mounted their mares, straddling them like a man and so unlike a proper English woman. We cantered through the village, retraced our path to the station, crossed the tracks, and began to gallop in the direction of the tavern and the cottage. About three hundred yards past the rail line we crossed a swollen river that was moving with great force from all the rain. The bridge seemed firm and I assumed that our three men had already crossed, so over we went and resumed our gallop.

As an officer in the medical core in Afghanistan I had been issued a horse and I was not unaware of how to ride. That was over thirty years ago and I had forgotten what a beating your knees and legs take as you strive to keep your body from bouncing on a saddle. I cursed the Jezreel bullet that had damaged my leg and forced me to grit my teeth against the pain, but I determined that there was no way under heaven that I would be out ridden by two women.

To my shock and wounded pride was added the further humiliation that these two women could ride like cavalry officers. They leaned forward, gripped the flanks of their mounts with their knees, took all the weight and movement into their legs and appeared to be of one substance with their excellent mares. Even though the legs of the beast were flying, hooves thundering, and powerful bodies surging with each leap forward, the heads of these women hardly moved an inch out of the horizontal plane. My God, was there anything these two could not do?

We approached the tavern, dismounted and entered. Our three men were already sitting at a table in the corner along with a portly man in an apron that I judged to be the barkeep. By their posture I could see that both Brett and Reggie were extremely impatient and anxious, but they were unfamiliar with the deliberate and patient methods of my friend and marvelous detective, Sherlock Holmes. He knew that friendly chat and a generous tip were an infinitely better way to encourage people to divulge all sorts of information than threats and bombast, and it was proving to have its effect on the proprietor of the establishment. We three sat down at the table next to them and Holmes introduced us with a comment on the excellent quality of the dark ale that had been served.

"Well sir, as I was sayin' sir, we saw those fellows off an on over the past three months, if you know what I mean. Right odd chaps they were. Foreigners they were. But not all from the same country which we knew from listenin' to them, if you know what I mean. One, the youngest fellow, hardly more than a school boy, was a sort of frenchie but maybe from Belgium. The father and his little fellow sounded like Russians but not quite if you know what I mean. At first we thoughts the little boy was only maybe a five year old but the way he talked and acted we thought he was maybe more like eight but just on the very small side, if you know what I mean. One of the others, the one with the beard, he was a German for sure and the last one, well now I just don't know. Somewhere else in Europe, meaning that he weren't no chinaman or such but none of us here could place his accent. They sat themselves in that table over there in the corner and kept to themselves not socializin' at all with the others in the village.

When they was talkin' they did so real quiet like, if you know what I mean, so that no one could hear what they talked about. But my Bessie she says that when she served them their food an such she heard them talkin' an they was talkin' English and that seemed like the only language that all had in common like. The little fellow, his father kept callin' him back to the table because he was wantin' to wander around an I can't blame him, if you know what I mean. So his father keeps callin' him Gavrilo or somethin' close to that. The young man, the frenchie, they called him Jean-Baptiste. The one who sounded Russian but wasn't, they call him Ivan, but we didn't catch any other names.

"We ask them, bein' friendly an all, what they was doin' in the village an they say they is studying our farming an especially our fertilizers. Well maybe that be true because they had some shipments of fertilizers shipped here an they come an picked them up an took them up to the cottage, but they never looked like the farmin' type, if you know what I mean. Most of my customers here, they're farmers and they got hands like meathooks, and big arms and red faces, and shoulders from workin' all their lives but these fellows they look more like the types that come around here from the government, or up from Cambridge. They were here up to a couple of weeks ago but then they left and we haven't seen hide nor hair of them since but Freddie, he's the owner of the cottage, he says that they paid their rent all in advance and their money's good enough for him so he don't ask any questions and just lets sleeping dogs lie if you know what I mean."

"My good man," said Holmes, "I think we understand exactly what you mean and we thank you for being so generous with the information on cottages to rent in the neighbourhood. We shall just have to look for another one if that one is spoken for. And we thank you for your excellent ale and look forward to our next enjoyable visit to your fine tavern. And now we must take our leave and be on our way."

"Always happy to serve some gentlemen and ladies especially those who is friendly like as you are. Most welcome back here anytime."

We rose and departed and mounted our horses. "If the cottage is vacant," I said, "Why are we going there. Should we not be trying to get to Bertie as quickly as we can?"

"Quite smart thinking, Watson," said Holmes, "except that the barkeep's reference to the fertilizer concerns me. There are many better ways to disguise their activities than pretending to be concerned with fertilizers and farming and certainly no need to have a shipment of it delivered if that is what is was. So we shall stop there for a quick inspection before trying to intercept the King's entourage on the way from Sandringham to the village. It has just gone eleven o'clock. We have sufficient time to stop them from shooting at him."

The cottage was a small private building with white walls and a thatched roof, a two-storied place with an old-fashioned porch and honeysuckle about it, well away from any other houses but pleasant and pretty enough. How galling that such a scenic location could be used to devise such demonic plans. The door was locked but Holmes quickly took care of that hindrance.

As soon as we entered I detected a strong smell, similar to the smell of a hospital ward after it had been cleaned and disinfected. Holmes smelt it too. He immediately, almost in a panic, began rifling through the detritus that was strewn through the cottage. Then he rushed outside and we heard him out the back of the building. He rushed back inside and shouted to us, "Come, we have not a second to spare. They are not going to shoot at the King. They have been making bombs."

Once he said that it was clear to me as well. What I had smelled was ammonia, the base for ammonium nitrate. Some called it the poor man's dynamite. In granular form it was quite stable, but when crushed to powder and combined with fuel oil it becomes highly explosive. It was used in the coal mines in Wales where the mining firms were too frugal and refused the additional expense of trinitrotoluene, the standard explosive of our wealthier English mining firms and of our military sappers.

The scraps of paper had many sheets that had been waxed. They were using them to wrap the explosive and keep it from getting damp.

"Behind the building, Holmes, what was there? Were there barrels that were used for delivery of chemicals?"

"There were at least a dozen of them; enough for a score of powerful bombs. Any one of them could blow the Prince's carriage to kingdom come. But let us divide and conquer. Watson, you stay here and inspect the cottage. Gather as much evidence as you can find that can be used when we drag these villains into court. Brett, Reggie and I will ride on and divert the King's procession. Fertilizer bombs are not like grenades that can be hurled. They are large and cumbersome and must be planted in place. If I can have the drivers change their route to the station we will foil these murderers."

The three of them rode off to the north, along the route to Sandringham. Miss Starlet and Miss Briany did not at all like being left out of the action and I had to remind them that more than half the time of a good detective or even a constable was always consumed with the paperwork. You could catch all the dastardly villains you wished but without evidence enough to convince a judge or jury they would never end up in a prison cell or swinging from the gallows. I said this of course to buoy up their spirits but inwardly I had to admit to myself that I too was annoyed with being left behind to do the work of the clerks. My annoyance was very short-lived.

"Do not move or we will kill you," said a voice from the doorway of the room. I turned quickly and saw two men, one with a swarthy beard, the other a youth. Both were armed and pointing revolvers at us.

"You fools. You should not have interfered. You are too late to do anything to save your King or your monstrous Empire. Now you will die along with your King and your husband, Mrs. Steward."

The older man was speaking. He had a thick German accent. I had my service revolver in my pocket but I could not reach for it quickly enough to do any good and doing so would imperil the lives of Briany and Miss Starlet. Yet if I did nothing I knew that these men had already killed and would not hesitate to do it, or worse, again. I had to find a way between Scylla and Charybdis. I gathered my wits and spoke back to them.

"Your plans are already foiled. Your bombs will go off on empty streets. You would be better to surrender and throw yourselves on the mercy of the courts and since no one has died you may be let off with just a few years in prison. Otherwise you will face the gallows. Please use your common sense."

Both of them laughed."Non, m'sieur," said the younger one, "I already have been along that path. I am free only because I was too young to be convicted for trying to kill your fat prince. Now I am older and I would be hung no matter what happens. So non, m'sier docteur Watson, we will leave no witnesses who know too much, and this time with the help of my comrades, I will succeed."

I looked at him closely and remembered the face from the papers of three years ago. Jean-Baptiste Sapido was only fifteen years old when he tried to kill the Prince of Wales as he was travelling through Belgium. He missed, was immediately apprehended, and put in jail. Because he was underage the Belgian courts let him walk free. He had returned, more ruthless, more fanatical than before, and had already helped to murder three men. My colleagues might be able to save the King but if I did not do something quickly this vile young man and his partner would soon be murdering me and these two women.

"You think we are so stupid that we put our bombs on roads"' said the older one with a sneer in his voice. "No, you fools. Roads can be so easily changed. Your railways cannot. In less than one hour the King of your greedy empire will have passed down the roadway to the cheers of your docile English peasants. He will then enter his lavish private railway car and his adoring subjects will watch as his body is blown into a thousand prices and spread across your green and pleasant countryside."

"Mrs. Steward, your husband and his friends have caused us a great deal of problems. But we cannot thank you enough for coming to England and identifying his associates for us. You made our task much easier. Now we shall have to teach a lesson to people like your husband and your idiot detective. The King will die but so will you. If we cannot kill your husband and son they will find your bodies violated and mutilated and no one will ever again doubt the determination of the Black Hand.

"Dr. Watson, sit in that chair," he motioned me towards a chair close to the table at the edge of the room. "Jean-Baptiste, give me your gun. I will keep two guns pointed at the breasts of these two women while you fasten Dr. Watson to the chair." With that the young man walked over to me, grabbed me by my shirt and pushed me forcefully into the chair. He picked up what I assumed was electrical wire that was used in making the caps for the bombs, forced my hands behind my back, lashed them painfully together and wound several strands of the wire around my torso. I was not able to move. Desperate despair had swept over me. Holmes would have ridiculed my prayer for divine intervention but I could see no other possibility for our lives and that of the King. A dark cloud was about to sweep across the civilised world. What I heard next added to the depths of my grief.

The young man then turned to the older one and said, "M'sieur, you are the senior man, which one do you wish? You may, of course, ravish the pretty blonde if you prefer. I will take the older one."

The bearded killer gave a vile laugh, "No, J-B, this older one is a rare beauty who has had many years to learn how to look after a man when she is on her knees and has a gun pointed at her head."

He looked at Miss Starlet and advanced towards her. Sure enough, once he was within the hand-to-hand combat zone the powerful leg and finely appointed boot rose rapidly and planted itself between his legs with an excruciating smack. Unlike the surly livery man the bearded one did not shout; he did not grasp at his groin or fall to the ground. He did not lower his gun. He merely staggered back, his body shaking with pain, and stood still until the pain subsided. He had obviously endured pain in the past and had disciplined himself to absorb it and keep fighting.

"Mrs. Steward, I admire your spirit. You are a fighter. So am I. As a professional courtesy I will cut off your breasts after I kill you and not before. But while you are alive I will violate every orifice of your body."

"Oh my," said Miss Starlet, "but you European men do disappoint me. All we hear in America is that you are supposed to be masters of physical love. You are the ones that know that the greatest satisfaction a man can have is when the woman is driven to distraction by his manhood. Please, sir, slow down, if this is to be my last time at least protect the reputation of your nation's men and make it an unforgettable one."

As she was speaking she was slowly lifting her skirt and exposing her leg. Briany kept watching Miss Starlet out of the corner of her eyes and copied her every move. "You want this, don't you," she was saying seductively to the younger killer. "You haven't seen a woman's leg before have you?" Her skirts were likewise lifting and exposing a very shapely thigh.

I was thoroughly confused. These two women stood a very good chance of being murdered and could be standing before Almighty God in a few minutes. Instead of committing the souls to their Maker they were behaving as if they were two-penny whores in the most disreputable of east end brothels.

"You're having trouble restraining yourself, aren't you?" Miss Starlet was saying to the older one. "I can tell you are. You want to take me and ravish me, don't you?" A few feet away Briany had started to caress her thigh and was making such conjugal sounds as should only ever be heard by a woman's husband during the throes of their honeymoon. Then Miss Starlet began making similar sounds as she moved her hand under her skirt.

Both men dropped their eyes from the faces of the women and began to fumble with the fronts of their trousers. In that short instant first Miss Starlet and a second later Briany removed their hands from their under their skirts, raised them quickly towards the faces of their would-be violators and I heard two pistol shots. Both men staggered back, dropped to their knees and toppled to the floor. The older one had a dark bloody hole where his nose had once been. The younger was starring at the ceiling with one lifeless eye as blood oozed out of the socket of the other one.

"Would you not agree, doctor," said Miss Starlet smiling in my direction, "that testosterone is truly one of the most dangerous chemicals known to man." She walked over towards Briany holding out her gun in the palm of her had.

"A Remington 41, double shot derringer. And yours?"

"The same, with the pearl handle? The ladies' model."

"How surprising. Mine exactly. Let me guess. A present for your twenty-fifth birthday."

"What a coincidence," Briany replied with a giggle. "You would think he could come up with some originality in the gifts he gives to the women in his life."

"So we might wish my dear. But let us not forget that while he is an exceptional man he is still . . ."

"*Just a man!*" they chorused in unison and then broke out into peels of girlish laughter.

"I do declare, honey child," said Miss Starlet, "I just might get to like having you as my daughter."

"Oh, now wouldn't that be lovely . . . *mommy.,*" said Briany with a merry giggle.

Miss Starlet's face took on a look of mock rage, "But not if you ever call me that again!" she said waging a finger in Briany's face.

"Sorry. Sorry. I promise. I promise. Miss Starlet. Miss Starlet," Briany sputtered in between laughter.

The two of them stopped laughing, looked intently at each other, and threw their arms around each other's shoulders.

"Ladies! Please!" I rebuked them. "We do not have time for this. Please. Untie me and let us move quickly. We must find the three men and get on with the task at hand. We have only a matter of minutes left before the bombs will explode." I confess that while I was exasperated with their girlish behaviour I was also dumbfounded that two women could have dispatched a couple of vile men a moment ago and immediately begin to chortle about their birthday presents.

"Pardon us, Dr. Watson," said Briany, as she undid the wire that bound my hands and body. "It's not every day that a girl gets to have her first ever adventure with her mother." In what was then an incongruous act of modesty the two of them turned their backs to me, lifted their skirts and replaced their derringers in the holsters that were strapped to their upper thighs.

"Very well," said Miss Starlet, "let us be on our way before this whole silly world goes to pieces yet again." We left the wretched bodies on the floor, quickly mounted our horses, and started off at a gallop to find the three men. We had only ridden north for a few minutes when we saw them in the distance approaching us. They were cantering along and seemed in no great concern. We met up with them and Holmes spoke first. "Disaster has been averted. We caught up with the procession north of the village and diverted their route. I am surprised, my dear Watson, that you have curtailed your investigation of the evidence so quickly…"

CHAPTER SEVEN - SAVING THE EMPIRE

"Holmes!" I screamed at him, but he ignored me and kept chattering away. "*Norbury* Holmes! *NORBURY!*" That got his attention and shut him up. I quickly explained about the location of the bombs. The story of the method employed by the two women to save civilization would have to wait. Alarm spread over the faces of the three men. Holmes looked at his watch.

"Good God," he cried, "we have only moments to spare before the King enters his car. Ride!"

"Horse," said Brett to his mount, "make tracks."

The six of us galloped south along the pathway. Again I cursed the Afghans but I did my best to keep up with the rest. Brett and Reggie pulled out in front as they did not hesitate to give their mounts hard kicks with the heels of their boots to spur them on. We thundered past the cottage, and then a few minutes later past the tavern and the barkeep who looked upon us with amazement from his doorway. Mentally I was calculating the vanishing time that was still available to us. If we could reach the bridge over the swollen river within the next five minutes we should have a grace period of yet another ten to reach the rail yard and the King's car. Lord willing we could do it. There was hope yet.

My moment of hope quickly vanished. Brett and Reggie had halted their horse in front of us and dismounted. The bridge was gone. The stream was over its banks, more than twenty yards separated us from the far side, and the waters were raging.

"No," I cried out, "It's been washed away. Yet it was firmly in place just an hour ago."

Holmes ran up to look at the remains of the structure. "It has not washed away. It has been destroyed by explosives. Yet again I have underestimated those evil men."

We could see the rail yard in the distance. It was no more than three hundred yards off. The King's car, the attached dining car, and the coach for his staff were all decked out with bunting and emblazoned with the coats of arms that only recently I could not recall. Any hope of anyone hearing our shouts was beyond praying.

"The next bridge is a quarter mile to the south," said Holmes. 'It is made of concrete and will still be in place. It is our only hope." He ran back to his horse, but stopped before mounting and turned to Briany. "Young lady, I believe I read that you took a prize in swimming." He looked at her face then deliberately turned his face towards the flooded river.

Briany looked puzzled for a brief moment, and then turned towards Reggie.

"Hey! Little brother!" she shouted at Reggie. "Can you swim?"

Reggie looked at her, puzzled for a moment, and then grinned. "I'll race you big sister!"

With that the two of them dropped their bodies to the grass and tugged off their boots. Briany stood up, ripped the buttons open on the bodice of her dress, shoved it back off her shoulders and let it fall to the ground. She stood before us in just her stocking feet, a white lace corset, and her undergarments. My inability to take my eyes off of her perfectly formed woman's body would demand an embarrassing time in confession.

Reggie took longer to strip out of his jacket, shirt and trousers but a moment later he was standing before us in just his briefs and socks, his arms and torso rippling and the muscles in his powerful thighs and calves magnificently defined.

"Father!" Briany shouted to Brett. "Throw our boots across!" Then she turned to her brother, "Let's go!"

First she and then her brother sprinted to the edge of the flooded stream and with a running dive entered the water. The powerful current swept both of their bodies downstream but with deliberate strokes each other them was moving steadily towards the far shore. We watched them, fearing for their safety until they were nearly fifty yards downstream but within a few feet of the distant bank.

Miss Starlet was watching them with a glow of parental pride. "Magnificent, aren't they doctor?"

While Miss Starlet gathered up her children's clothes, Brett picked up the two pairs of boots. Sherlock Holmes placed a hand on his arm and said, "Pardon me sir. But there are a few things at which an English schoolboy excels."

He took one of the boots at the top of the upper, ran back about ten yards and with rapid strides ran towards the edge of the river. A few steps before reaching the corner his long thin arm began to move in a full circle with the boot firmly in his grasp. As he reached the water's edge the circle of his arm reached its apex and he let the boot fly – as good of a cricket toss as I have ever seen. The boot soared through the air and landed in the grass well beyond the far edge of the river. He repeated the feat another three times and all four boots were hurled to the other shore.

"I reckon that your game of cricket is not as uselss as I thought," mused Brett.

"In my youth I dispatched many a batter and won my share of sticky wickets," said Holmes.

On the far shore the young athletes had climbed out the water and run back to fetch their boots. Quickly they dropped to the grass and tugged their boots back on to their feet. "Hey there! I won!" shouted Briany back at us. "Not fair!" shouted Reggie, "she had a head start!"

They rose, turned towards the rail yard and began sprinting down the gravel road at a speed that only the runners in our recent Olympic Games could have matched.

"Move it!" Brett shouted to us. "We have to ride to that next bridge try to get to the car before it blows."

We remounted and galloped hard to the south. The concrete bridge was still firm. We crossed it and turned back to the north. In the distance we could see the rail yard and the air above it was still clear with no sign of smoke of flame. We had closed the distance to less than one hundred yards when an enormous explosion shook the earth. The horses halted and reared up on their back legs in fear. We struggled not to fall off and looked back at what had been the royal railway car. There were flames in many places. The superstructure of the King's private car was entirely gone. All that was left was the base. Debris was scatted for yards around and thick smoke was billowing from the site. We could hear screams of distress coming from the platform at the far end.

A sickening feeling crept over me. I looked at Holmes who looked back at me. "My dear friend," he said, "a prayer might be in order."

We dismounted and walked towards the chaos with our handkerchiefs covering our mouths to protect us from the acrid fumes. I placed my hand on Holmes's arm and we plodded our way forward, fearing the worst. Behind us were Brett and Miss Starlet. She had slipped her arm through his and was holding it tightly. They knew that their children had more than enough time to reach the car before the explosion. They also knew that no life could have survived.

As we reached what was left of the car we stepped over the pieces of furniture, partitions, and toilet fixtures that were strewn on the ground and down the embankment. Holmes moved back from the car and began to look into the debris that surrounded it. He did not have to tell me what he was doing. I knew that human bodies are dense and even in violent explosions do not move far from where they have been prior situated. Holmes had begun his search for what were the remains of our King and our children. Silently I followed him. Brett and Miss Starlet followed me. She was still holding tightly to his arm.

From the base of the embankment a familiar voice called out. "Yoohoo! Mommy! Daddy! Over here!" Thank God. They were alive. Staggering up the embankment were our two young heroes, clad only in their underwear and scratched and muddied flesh. Between them and being held on each side was a stout bearded man in military trousers and a white shirt that was untucked at his ample waist.

Miss Starlet burst into tears of joy and relief. Brett Steward handed her his handkerchief.

We met them as they reached to top of the hill. Holmes and I knew that British etiquette did not permit us to throw hugs and kisses on children in the presence of the King of England, but being Americans Brett and Miss Starlet practised no such restraint. That being done, Brett turned to the dishevelled man and said, "Hello there Bertie. Thought I would drop in on your party. I see you have already met my family." He nodded in the direction of the scantily clothed young man and woman.

Prince Albert Edward, soon to be King Edward VII of England, looked at us without a word and then said, "Come and see me next week at Buckingham" and then walked off towards the station, tucking his shirt back into his trousers as he went.

" Umm . . . Father," said Reggie, "could you look up to the top of the station? On the roof. Through the smoke."

We all looked up. Holmes pulled out his spyglass, looked briefly and handed it to Brett. He looked for a brief moment, gave the glass back and unslung his rifle from behind his back.

Through the smoke we could make out three figures on the station roof. There were two men. One sat by himself. The other had a child sitting beside him. We watched them closely while the King made his way past the third railway car and rounded the far end of the staff coach. We heard a roar of cheers from the railway platform as the crowd of villagers discerned that it was the King and that he was safe and sound.

The man who was sitting alone quickly jumped to his feet. He appeared to be looking down into the crowd and then he bent over and picked up a rifle and lifted it to his shoulder.

"No sir," said Brett quietly, "I don't think you're going to do that." He quickly sighted the gun and pulled the trigger.

The Mauser gave a sharp crack and we could see the man fall back. The other man leapt to his feet ran over to the where the shooter had been standing, then immediately ran back, picked up the child and disappeared out of our sight over the back end of the roof.

"You are a fine shot sir," said Holmes. "Well done."

"I did have some practice a few years back shooting Yankees," said Brett. "Some things you just don't forget."

"Nor, I suspect," responded Holmes, "shall that man and his son forget what they came to do. I fear we have not heard the last from little Gavrilo and his father."

"Well sir, we have certainly heard the last of them today," said Starlet, "so we can put all this behind us until the next silly war breaks out. And gentleman, I do declare, that riding has given me an appetite. I cannot imagine that this village serves barbeque and mint juleps but I am sure our great detective can find us some place to relax ourselves."

"I am sure that is quite possible, Miss Starlet," said Holmes. "My notes tell me that there is a decent pub close by. It is reported to be spotless and, if you can ignore the grumpy publican and condition of the WC's as a result of litigation with the next door neighbour, acceptably convivial. If we make our way there quickly we should be able to get served before the madding crowd descends on it."

Miss Starlet looked sternly at the nearly naked young man and woman, "Great balls of fire. What am I going to do with you two? Your clothes are back with the horses. If you will get dressed and promise to behave yourselves your mother and father will treat you to lunch." She struggled to get the last few words out before breaking into a joyful laugh.

"Best offer I had all morning," said Reggie, "I'm hungry enough to eat a horse. How about you, father?"

"And wash it down with a cold beer, if only they had such a thing in this backward nation," replied Brett.

EPILOGUE

In a corner of the *Crown and Mitre* we sat and talked in quiet tones, struggling to be heard over the boisterous voices of the patrons who it seemed all had their own version of the events of the day and all had to repeat their stories to all their neighbours.

Reggie had dutifully made several trips to the bar and returned to our table bearing plates of hot battered cod, chips and mushy peas, four ales, and two shandies for the ladies.

"So let's hear you tell us," said Brett to his son and daughter, "how it was you managed to rescue my ol' pal, Bertie, the King of England."

"We ran," began Briany, "pell mell towards the car. We knew by the station clock tower that the King was already inside it. We tried the doors on our side but they were firmly locked. Reggie saw that one of the car windows was open and that the space was large enough for me to fit through, so he hoisted me up and into it. I ran back straightaway to the door and unlocked it so he could enter. We ran up and down through the car but it was empty. We could see no one at all. But then my brother had a brilliant idea."

"I had heard," Reggie continued, "that the King was enormously fond of food and drink and as any man knows that means that he must also have to spend a lot of time on the loo. So I ran towards one WC at the north end of the car while my sister ran to the other end. Mine was empty but she…"

"I opened the door and there he was. The almost king of England sitting on his throne. I shouted down the car to Reggie and then turned my attention to his Highness. I must say he was looking at me very oddly. 'Sir,' I said, 'You must get out of here at once!' and he just laughed at me. 'Bloody hell!' he shouted, 'such a lovely parting gift from the villagers. But surely you can wait a moment until I have finished in here'. He has, it would appear earned his reputation as a cad and a somewhat crude bon vivant. Then Reggie appeared and again the king laughed. 'One of each,' he shouted, 'God bless these villagers of King's Lynn. But my dear boy just wait for me in the bedchamber and I will be there in three royal minutes.' 'Sir,' I said, 'You don't understand, your life is in danger. We have to get you out of here.' Reggie and I gave each other a look and then he said to the King . . ."

"I said, 'Sorry Bertie old sport, but it's time to move.' So I grabbed him under one arm, my sister grabbed the other and we man-handled him off the loo, out of the WC, and out of the door of the car. We all fell in a heap on the gravel beside the track. He was bellowing very nasty curses at us by this time but we pulled him forward and pushed him down the embankment. He is fat and awkward and so he rolled like a beer barrel to the bottom. We ran down and flattened our bodies on top of his."

"Then the car exploded," said Briany. "We were protected, being at the bottom of the embankment. The force and the projectiles flew over our heads. We stayed in place for a couple of minutes but once we realized that there was going to be no secondary blast we got up off of Bertie, helped him to his feet, pulled up his trousers, and made sure that he was unharmed. I looked up then and saw you. And here we are."

"Yes my dears, here we are for sure," said Brett, "and unless I am sorely mistaken the world will never hear of what you did unless Dr. Watson here tells them and even then they may not believe us."

"Ah, so true," said Holmes. "But you will know in your hearts that you have defeated the forces of unspeakable evil. But you must tell us, dear ladies, how you managed to shoot two very disciplined anarchists at close range."

"Fiddle-dee-dee, Sherlock," returned Miss Starlet, "there are some things that ever the great detective is better off not knowing."

A week passed during which we all made our reports to Scotland Yard and Whitehall. The bodies of the three anarchists were removed from the cottage and the station, identified, and secretly buried. The name of the man who escaped remained unknown. We knew the child only by his Christian name of Gavrilo.

Another rail car was found for the King and he made his way first to Windsor, then Buckingham, and on Saturday, August 9, in the year of our Lord 1902, Albert Edward, the oldest son of Queen Victoria and the Prince Consort was crowned King of England, Sovereign of the British Empire, and Emperor of India. The crowds cheered.

On August the fifteenth we gathered in a small room in the Palace for a private ceremony. His Highness said a few perfunctory words of gratitude but then added, "As none of you are members of our Empire's armed forces I cannot award you the Cross that bears my mother's name. But your valour is every bit deserving of it and shall not be forgotten." For a moment he looked quite directly into the face of Briany. She raised her hand to her mouth and with her thumb and first finger gently pinched her lips together. The King gave a very small smile and nod and we were ushered out. Momma was waiting for us.

" 'Bout times y'all get done. So did dat fat boy what was all trussed up in buttons and bows give you some trinkets seeins how y'all jus 'bout got yoursells all blow up savin' him? But ah 'spects thuh angels was fightin' on yor side. Buts y'all know doan you dat we got fat boys in Ayatlanta what'll give yooz trinkets. We call boys like dat damn Yankees."

I believe I caught a quick flash of a brilliant red petticoat beneath her modest black skirt.

Over a celebratory tea at Claridges Miss Starlet announced, "We have sent telegrams to Atlanta and have arranged to have a true Southern party on the fifteenth of September to celebrate our family reunion and to send Reggie off to the Citadel. We will be serving barbeque to all of the best and brightest of Atlanta and we simply must have you, Sherlock Holmes, and you John Watson with us to be part of it. We will arrange to book you first class passage on Cunard's new steamship and entertain you as only those born, by the grace of God, in the South can do. I will not hear otherwise, you are coming to America."

"No, my dear Miss Starlet, we are doing no such thing," said Holmes kindly but firmly. "Evil men are still at large and planning unspeakable deeds and I have no choice but to continue my singular pursuit and defeat of them. So I must with gratitude decline your gracious offer."

"No Sherlock."

"Yes, Starlet."

"No Sherlock!"

"Yes, Starlet."

"But it just won't be a complete celebration without you. I shall be totally devastated. My feelings will be crushed. You will spoil my time eating barbeque. What will I do?" Her face dawned her famous pout.

Holmes gave her an imperious look and, with just the hint of a wink at Brett, responded,

"Frankly my dear, I don't give a damn."

ABOUT THE AUTHOR

Once upon a time Craig Stephen Copland was an English major and studied under both Northrop Frye and Marshall McLuhan at the University of Toronto way back in the 1960's. He never got over his spiritual attraction to great literature and captivating stories. Somewhere in the decades since he became a Sherlockian. He is a recent member of the Bootmakers of Toronto (www.torontobootmakers.com), and mildly addicted to the sacred canon. In real life he writes about and serves as a consultant for political campaigns in Canada and the USA (www.ConservativeGrowth.net) , but would abandon that pursuit if he could possibly earn a decent living writing about Sherlock Holmes.

OTHER NEW SHERLOCK HOLMES MYSTERIES BY CRAIG STEPHEN COPLAND

www.SherlockHolmesMystery.com

Available from Amazon as either ebook or paperback.

The Man Who Was Twisted But Hip. It is 1897. Dr. Watson is sent on a mission to the East End to rescue his wayward nephew. He encounters Sherlock Holmes and the two of them are plunged into an international plot that could bring chaos to all of Europe.

France is torn apart by the Dreyfus Affair. Westminster needs help from Sherlock Holmes to make sure that the tide of anti-Semitism will not spread to England. A young officer in the Foreign Office suddenly resigns his post and joins the theater. His wife seeks help from Sherlock Holmes. The evil professor is up to something, and it could have terrible consequences for the young couple and for conflict among nations. Holmes and Watson must go to Paris, solve the puzzle, and thwart Moriarty.

The Bald-Headed Trust. Watson insists on taking Sherlock Holmes on a short vacation to the seaside in Plymouth. No sooner has Holmes arrived than he is needed to solve a double murder and prevent a massive fraud diabolically designed by the evil Professor himself. Who knew that a family of devout conservative churchgoers could come to the aid of Sherlock Holmes and bring enormous grief to evil doers? The story is inspired by *The Red-Headed League,* one of the original stories in the canon of Sherlock Holmes by Sir Arthur Conan Doyle.

A Scandal in Fordlandia. Another parody- this one inspired by *A Scandal in Bohemia* and set in Toronto in 2014. Sherlock Holmes and Dr. Watson are visited by Toronto's famous (infamous?) mayor. When he was a teenager someone took some nasty photos of him and if they are made public, disaster could come not only upon those in the photo but on all of civilization as we know it. Holmes and Watson must retrieve the photos before they are printed in the unfriendly press.

The Hudson Valley Mystery. A young man in New York went mad and murdered his father. His mother knows he is innocent and knows he is not crazy. She appeals to Sherlock Holmes and together with Dr. and Mrs. Watson he crosses the Atlantic to help this client in need. Once there they must duel with the villains of Tammany hall and with the specter of the legendary headless horseman. Inspired by *The Buscombe Valley Mystery*.

A Case of Identity Theft. It is the fall of 1888 and Jack the Ripper is terrorizing London. A young married couple are found, minus their heads. Another young couple is missing and in peril. Sherlock Holmes, Dr. Watson, the couple's mothers, and Mycroft must join forces to find the murderer before he kills again and makes off with half a million pounds. The novella is inspired by *A Case of Identity* and the text of the original Sherlock Holmes story is included in the paperback version.

The Sign of the Third. Fifteen hundred years ago the courageous Princess Hemamali smuggled the sacred tooth of the Buddha into Ceylon. Since that time it has never left the Temple of the Tooth in Kandy, where it has been guarded and worshiped by the faithful. Now, for the first time, it is being brought to London to be part of a magnificent exhibit at the British Museum. But what if something were to happen to it? It would be a disaster for the British Empire. Sherlock Holmes, Dr. Watson and even Mycroft Holmes are called upon to prevent such a crisis. Will they prevail? What is about to happen to Dr. John Watson? And who is this mysterious young Irregular they call The Injin? This novella is inspired by the Sherlock Holmes mystery, *The Sign of the Four*. The same characters and villains are present, and fans of Arthur Conan Doyle's Sherlock Holmes will enjoy seeing their hero called upon yet again to use his powers of scientific deduction to thwart dangerous and dastardly criminals. The text of the original story, *The Sign of the Four*, is included in the paperback version. Your enjoyment of the book will be enhanced by re-reading the Sherlock Holmes classic and then seeing what new adventures are in store.

The Mystery of the Five Oranges. On a miserable rainy evening a desperate father enters 221B Baker Street. His daughter has been kidnapped and spirited off the North America. The evil network who have taken her have spies everywhere. If he goes to Scotland Yard they will kill her. There is only one hope – Sherlock Holmes.

Holmes and Watson sail to a small corner of Canada, Prince Edward Island, in search of the girl. They find themselves fighting one of the most powerful and malicious organizations on earth – the Ku Klux Klan. But they are aided in their quest by the newest member of the Baker Street Irregulars, a determined and imaginative young redhead, and by the resources of the Royal Canadian Mounted Police.

Sherlockians will enjoy this new adventure of the world's most famous detective, inspired by the original story of The Five Orange Pips. And those who love Anne of Green Gables will thrill to see her recruited by Holmes and Watson to help in the defeat of crime.

Sherlock and Barack. This is NOT a new Sherlock Holmes Mystery. It is a Sherlockian research paper seeking answers to some very serious questions. Why did Barack Obama win in November 2012? Why did Mitt Romney lose? Pundits and political scientists have offered countless reasons. This book reveals the real reason - The Sherlock Holmes Factor. Had it not been for Sherlock Holmes, Mitt Romney would be president. This study is the first entry by Sherlockian Craig Stephen Copland into the Grand Game of amateur analysis of the canon of Sherlock Holmes stories, and their effect on western civilization. Sherlockians will enjoy the logical deductions that lead to the inevitable conclusions. A full copy of *A Study in Scarlet*, the story responsible for the November 2012 Sherlock Holmes Factor, is included in this book so that novice readers may confront the evidence and decide for themselves.

Made in the USA
Middletown, DE
19 April 2015